The Nemesis Circle

By

M.E. Martin

Prologue

The article on page four of the Glasgow Herald read:

"Yesterday, Friday 1st May, a man was knocked down and fatally injured on Great Western Road.

He was later identified as Simon McKenzie, age 24 years."

There was no warning in this brief report of the havoc that this single act of crass stupidity would cause.

No hint of the far-reaching change within a mother who, driven by an obsessive need for vengeance, further fuelled by a deadly resolve, would go to any lengths in her elusive search for vengeance.

The difference between justice and revenge is a fine line to tread. . .

Chapter One

Ursula McKenzie was glad to be home. Glancing around her neat living room, glad now she had chosen to please herself by buying a cream linen look suite, the coloured cushions were a cheerful addition, bright and fresh, she thought. As she waited for the kettle to boil, the doorbell rang. It was more than likely her wee neighbour, Mrs Reid, needing a favour. She opened the door to find three men filling the doorway.

"Are you Mrs McKenzie?" one asked pleasantly.

She was a little apprehensive but she stood back to let them in, smiling inwardly as she thought how big they looked in her small hallway.

"My name is Detective Sergeant Andrew McNeil, and these gentlemen are my colleagues, Constable Ian Dunn and James Lang," he said, gesturing towards the men. She motioned them to come into the living room and sit down. As they did so his face took on a more serious expression.

"Could you tell me, Mrs McKenzie, do you have a son, Simon?"

"Yes I do," she replied. At that she felt a cold shiver down her spine.

"Mrs McKenzie, I'm afraid I have some very bad news for you. There has been an accident, involving a car, involving your son Simon. I am very sorry to inform you, Simon died at the scene."

He motioned her to sit down.

"I don't understand," she said, "it can't be my Simon. I spoke to him yesterday afternoon," she stammered out.

"This incident happened last night and we only traced you this morning," said Sergeant Andrew McNeil.

Ursula sat motionless, light-headed and silent. She stared at the three men.

"It can't be my Simon, I spoke to him yesterday afternoon," she stammered.

"This incident happened last night and we only traced you this morning," he replied gently.

Ursula's heart was hammering in her chest. Her brain had stopped functioning. She could not speak, as harsh sobs stuck in her throat. She was in some kind of fog. Hot tears slid down her face as she looked at them. They were looking at her strangely as if they knew she was not with them.

Suddenly the older one spoke, "Are you all right Mrs McKenzie?" he asked kindly. Ursula was not all right, she was all wrong, as if she had been turned to stone. At the same time she wanted to run and run.

"Mrs McKenzie, is there anyone we can phone to be with you?"

"Yes, yes, my daughter, Ruth. Oh no, she might not be home from work yet."

"Just give us the number. We'll contact her. Does she live far from here?" he asked.

"Ten minutes away. She won't know about Simon yet, someone will have to tell her. Oh God, she will be devastated, he is her baby brother," she added.

"You leave that to us. Is the number in this book?" he asked, pointing to a small book lying beside the phone. He glanced towards the other man.

"We'll leave Constable Lang here with you as he is a Family Liaison Officer. He will answer any questions you may have. Another thing, Mrs McKenzie, someone will have to formally identify your son."

She looked up at him in confusion, reality starting to dawn on her. How was he to know her whole world was now in tatters?

"Maybe, my ex-husband, his father, would do that for us," she said in a high-pitched voice.

"Yes fine, if you give us his address and phone number, we will do the rest. These things take a few days to organise. We are so sorry for your loss and understand, Mrs McKenzie, it is quite a lot to take in at the moment," he stated, inclining his head towards her, a small smile of sympathy at his mouth.

Both men stood up, expressing their condolences as they left. The remaining policeman closed the door behind them.

"I'll make us both a cup of tea," he said, briskly heading towards the kitchen. "Then we will discuss what is the best way to help you through this. We will do anything we can." Numbly, she dropped onto the sofa, confused, her mind in a turmoil. One hour ago, she had been a normal, happy person. Now, she asked herself, could she not visualise Simon as the man he was? She could only see him as a bright three-year-old, as he ran towards her, arms outstretched, calling out, "Mummy, Mummy," his face wreathed in smiles. God help me. What am I going to do? How the blazes will I get through this? My clever darling boy. Gone forever. She could not even cry, though tears may have helped. Was she not even to be granted that small relief?

Chapter 2

The man responsible for Simon's death had been apprehended at home, within hours of the incident.

Matt Thomson paced up and down the police interview room. Christ, he was in deep shit this time. He should never have left the scene of the accident. Not a clever move that, he thought. Then when he arrived home in a blind panic his wife had been a right fucking pain. He had really needed that wee half, but clever clogs had snatched it from him and poured it down the sink. Imagine! Twelve-year-old whisky. Then to make matters even worse, she had phoned the polis. Who the hell did she think she was, fucking Rebus?

She knew fine well it would get him into all kinds of trouble. What she needed was a right good, hard slap, so she did. She had warned him the last time, if it happened again he was on his own. Well, that suits me and good riddance. That last lawyer had cost a fortune. Bad enough, fuck! But this time, the guy had been killed. He should have been faster on the pedestrian crossing. This was going to cost an arm and a leg.

All she worried about was the neighbours, who the bloody hell worried about them? Right enough, the afront of it, taken from the house in handcuffs into a police car. Then the breath and urine test. Treating me like a fucking criminal, I ask you. Still, that young polis said it was the lowest one that counted. Hey, with a bit of luck I might not have been over the limit. Shit. Fat chance.

Bugger, I didn't mean to stay as long at the club, but you get talked into having one or two extra nips. Christ, it was big Charlie's birthday after all.

Outside in the corridor he could hear raised voices. What the hell was going on out there? Someone was in worse trouble than him. Some chemical not being changed. His voice getting louder.

"These things should not be left to inexperienced members of staff. Midnight on Sunday is too difficult to understand? Hell's bells, some bloody people have the IQ of a tomato plant." He paused for breath then continued, even louder. "Do you realise the ramifications of this mess? These readings tell us how much alcohol is in their blood. Without them we cannot prosecute, damn! Bottom line is we can't use any readings from last Sunday until today. Just get out of my bloody sight!" He heaved an exasperated sigh.

Silence.

Christ that guy is gonna have a stroke if he goes on much more, he thought. But that's a wee gem to keep in mind for a lawyer. Anyway, much more important, where the hell were they bloody polis, they've got a nerve keeping me here this long?

"Hey guys, my time is up and I am as sober as a judge," he shouted.

At that, the policeman came to let him go home.

"Thank Christ," he said. "Somebody having a wee temper tantrum," he sniggered.

"Move now!" the policeman roared.

Chapter 3

As usual, Ursula lay in bed, sleepless. Her mind drifted back to Simon's funeral. Her ex-husband, James, had identified his body. She shuddered at the thought and, the next day, he'd come to the house.

"Ursula, would you like me to arrange the funeral?" he asked. "Tell me what you would like and I'll deal with it," he said kindly.

She remembered telling him to go ahead, adding sadly, "I don't think I could cope, James. But even if he is cremated I want him to have a proper grave with a headstone and his name."

"No bother," he replied.

There had been a short service at the crematorium, followed by a meal somewhere. It had all passed before her like a film, not real, but it was real, she thought. There had been so many young people.

"So very sorry, Mrs McKenzie," they said, each and every one in tears while she stood, dry-eyed and silent. She remembered some of them from Simon's school days.

Suddenly, she heard sobbing from the next bedroom. It would be Ruth. God help her, she thought. Putting on her dressing gown, she slipped in beside her.

"It's all right, Ruth, I'm here," she told her.

"Oh, Mum," she sobbed. "I will never get over losing my little brother. It is all so senseless. Why?" she whimpered.

Ursula could only hold her closer, thinking to herself, this is bloody hell, watching my girl incoherent with grief. Holding her even closer as her own tears dripped down her chin.

"Ruth, tomorrow we will have a day off. A walk in the park. More importantly, a good long talk."

Next morning saw them in the park, a bright, fresh day, just the kind of day for turning over a new leaf. Ursula laid out her proposal.

"Ruth, tomorrow you will go back to your own flat, pick up your life and friends. We can only cry between midnight and six in the morning. Moreover, we will paint our smiles on with our lipstick. We are miserable and our misery makes other people sad. So, come on Ruth, Simon would not want this for us." She squeezed Ruth's hand.

"Mum," said Ruth, giving her mother a look of gratitude, "you are a treasure, you always know what's best for us."

Now back at work, Ursula was beginning to pick up the threads of a – now – different life. She appeared to her friends to be quieter. It was on a Sunday about a month later, she got her first inkling of the storms to come. She had invited Peter and his wife, Sarah, friends of long-standing, and Robbie and his girlfriend, Lucy, who had been friends of Simon's, for lunch.

The meal was a cheerful affair until, quite unexpectedly, Robbie said, "That guy who was involved in Simon's accident had been drunk and was to be sent to the High Court in Glasgow."

This was news to Ursula and Ruth and it took a minute to sink in.

"What do you mean he was drunk?" she queried. "How can you know this, Robbie?"

"Well, he was well over the limit; also it was not his first offence." Oh, hell, he thought, I should have kept my mouth shut. I was told this in confidence.

Ursula could sense his embarrassment and looked at him coldly, but wordless.

"Well, I hope he gets the maximum jail time; it's about fourteen years," said Ruth.

"Not if he gets a really smart lawyer who can have the charges reduced. Then he only gets a very large fine!" Peter persisted.

"It will cost him a packet," said Lucy, trying desperately to change the subject. "Are you back at work now, Ursula?" she asked brightly, at the same time giving Robbie a hard stare.

Ursula's calm exterior belied the white-hot rage welling up inside her. She made up her mind. Tomorrow she would phone the police and ask for an interview with a senior officer.

Her appointment the following week helped to reassure her. The Chief Constable, Neil Frazer, understood her concerns.

"I was not told that the driver who killed my son was drunk and this is not his first offence," she said bitterly. "And there is a chance he will get off with a large fine," she went on.

"Mrs McKenzie, drunk drivers who cause a fatality do not get off, as you say, with a fine. This is an offence of the utmost gravity and, as such, would merit a severe penalty." He paused. "Yes, I understand there are specialised road traffic lawyers and solicitors who would take these cases. However, in this case it is a repeat offence and, as such, would be dealt with in the High Court, in Glasgow."

Well, she told herself, feeling a small sense of relief, he should know. Tomorrow, I will go to that bereavement counsellor in Glasgow. That might make me feel a bit better.

Chapter 4

The day Ursula had longed for and dreaded equally had arrived. Nothing could have prepared her for the court case. She could not control her trembling knees. Having never been in a court room before, let alone a High Court, she was quite intimidated by the quiet buzz going on around her.

James, who had accompanied her, warned in a whisper, "These cases can be quite long and drawn out, Ursula, so be prepared."

"That's fine," she answered, "I haven't got a clue but I will pay attention. Where will that man, Thomson, be sitting?"

"Yes, of course, he will be in the dock." He pointed out where it was.

At that, Ruth appeared, slightly out of breath.

"So sorry, Mum and Dad. I could not leave you to face this ordeal on your own," she murmured, linking her arm through her mother's.

Ursula was overwhelmed at the sight of all those lawyers, or were they solicitors, or QCs, en masse, so to speak?

"How do you tell the difference, James?"

He pointed out the prosecuting counsel. Or maybe he was the Advocate Depute, saying, "Just remember him. He is the one who is on our side."

Surprisingly, they all seemed to know one another. She saw small nods of recognition pass amongst them. Ursula glanced at Ruth.

"There seems to be an awful lot of people in here. Are they witnesses, or maybe they are his family here to give him a bit of Dutch courage?" she surmised.

"By God, he will need it. That man is going to be punished for my brother's death," answered Ruth bitterly and, under her breath, "little rat!"

"He deserves life but fourteen years will do well enough," she replied.

The judge came in and everybody stood up.

A lawyer was reading out the charges. Dangerous driving, no mention of Simon being killed.

What the hell!

Then Thomson's lawyer, Campbell McIntosh, stood up. She could not make out clearly what he said.

Suddenly, there were gasps of disbelief, lawyers whispering to each other. Detectives at the back seemed shocked, looking around, as lost as she felt. What the hell was happening, she thought.

Then the judge said in a loud voice, "I am dismissing this case due to a procedural error. As the defence stated, the police case was inadmissible in evidence. Therefore, I have no alternative as there is no case to answer." He looked at Thomson coldly.

"You may go."

There was utter confusion throughout the court. What did he mean?

She saw James lower his head in his hands, sobbing.

"Oh my God, my God, my son," he cried.

In all her married life, she had never seen him cry. Hardly believing what she was seeing, she laid her hand on his shoulder.

Turning to Ruth, she said, "Your father said it would take a while. To my mind, it was over almost before it started. Whatever that McIntosh said changed everything."

Ursula looked over James's head, towards Ruth, who was looking at her uncomprehendingly.

"What happened, Mum? Did that murdering shitbag just get off murdering my baby brother?" Tears stole down Ruth's cheeks.

"I don't know," sobbed Ursula. "The police said he would go to prison," she answered plaintively.

Gathering himself together, James took both their arms, ushering them towards the door.

"Come on. We'll get you two home. There is nothing we can do here," he uttered brokenly.

Chapter 5

Later that day, as all three sat in shock and dumb despair, the doorbell rang. Ursula opened the door to find two policemen on the step.

"May we come in, Mrs McKenzie?" one asked politely.

She motioned for them to enter and take a seat.

"My name is Detective Inspector John Diamond. I believe you already know DS Andrew McNeil."

All three stared back at them grimly.

"We have been asked by the Chief Constable, Neil Frazer, to speak to you," he said. "He thought you were due an explanation of this morning's events," continuing. "To put it simply, the machine we use to take alcohol breath or urine counts uses a chemical, ethanol, which is changed at midnight each Sunday. Unfortunately, a civilian member of staff forgot to change the chemical that day." He paused to let them absorb this knowledge.

"As a result, the week's counts could not be used, thus could not be used in evidence. Matt Thomson's tests were included in those counts." He paused.

"In addition, while he was being detained, he overheard this matter being discussed and told his lawyer, Campbell McIntosh, who moreover, told the judge. It was a procedural error so could not be used in evidence against him. The judge has then no alternative but to dismiss the case against him."

James interrupted him. "Are you telling me it was police negligence that caused this whole debacle? We are talking about my son, my only son, and not someone's pet cat," he snapped bitterly.

"We cannot say how sorry we are about this. You will, of course, receive a formal letter of apology from the Chief Constable," he continued.

"Tell him not to bother," interjected Ruth rudely.

After that, they got up to leave, once again giving their condolences, leaving James, Ursula and Ruth to sit and ponder.

Turning to James and Ruth, Ursula spattered out, "Why do they keep calling it an accident? It was downright murder. The minute a drunk person gets behind the wheel of a car, he is a potential killer." Her voice was raising with temper. "The police can't do much as their hands are tied by duplicitous politicians who cannot or will not address the problem. Lawyers use drunk driver trials as a game! One in which the most deceitful and despicable wins. I have been online and it would turn your stomach."

She went on. "Drunk drivers are seen throughout the law profession as the best money spinner in the world. They rub their hands with glee as those creeps enter their doors."

Ruth and James tried in vain to calm her down.

A tiny seed of vengeance and hatred was planted deep in Ursula McKenzie that day. Not so much to grow as to fester.

Chapter 6

Matt Thomson was stunned! He sat in the club with a pint. I'll pass on the shorts the'day, he thought.

He could hardly believe that wee bit of news he had told the lawyer had got him off. Maybe I'll get a discount? Fat chance. It had taken the bugger all his time to say thanks as he handed over a cheque for ten grand. Not even a handshake as he left the court. Christ! If she knew what it had cost, there would be hell. He was one smarmy git, that McIntosh guy, thought Matt.

"How to get away with murder," ran the headline, and all the gory details on the inside pages. What about that hellish photo, pound to a penny that bitch had given it to them. She had been hoping he would be put away for a few years. Well, hard cheese her, he sneered. Yet he seemed to be getting the, *Hi Matt,* then guys moving on, here today.

Right enough, he felt sorry for the guy's parents. But he was dead and you sure as hell canny come back. Anyway, to hell with them all. I will book a wee break in Spain or Portugal. I need to get away for a while from her. She'll be like a fucking fiend, so she will. He consoled himself with thoughts of a wee break.

Chapter 7

Ursula sat in her favourite armchair mulling over all that had happened. *Think rationally*, she scolded herself. She had not got any justice from the justice system or any help from anyone. She had decided in her quest for normality she would go to the bereavement class in town. Two evenings a week might help.

However, her mind was in utter turmoil. Her nights were an action replay of Simon's funeral while her days were filled with blind hatred and revenge. The police had been no help at all. These bloody lawyers could run rings around them, even she could see that. She would have to come up with a plan, one that would work.

She had plenty of money but she did not know anyone so that was out. This required secrecy. When Ursula's mother had passed, she had willed her three-bedroom flat in the West End to Ruth and Simon. She had lived there for thirty years or more. They could not believe the amount it was worth. Ruth had bought her wee flat and car with her share but Simon had left his in the bank. As he shared his flat with two mates, his intention was to buy somewhere when he'd seen what he wanted. Simon had left his mother a tidy sum. Her house and car were paid. Her own salary and a pension when she retired.

She was determined to get her act together, sort out her muddled mind. At the same time, she would put a plan in motion. Matt Thomson would be paid in full. I don't know how or when, but he will, she reassured herself. That thought made her feel better already. Her two evenings at bereavement would start this Monday, and bugger, she thought, I'm going.

There were quite a few people at the class. All seemed friendly. Also, after the talk, tea and coffee were served. Ursula sat beside a young woman.

"My name is Maddie," she said.

"I'm Ursula. Is this your first time here?"

"No, I've been once before. I promised my mother I would come, so here I am."

"This is my first time and I promised myself I would come. For the simple reason, I cannot cope. My mind is in a constant mess. Are you the same, Maddie?"

"Well, I would say more than a mess. Bordering on insanity if I'm honest," she replied.

As they left to go home, they both knew they had found a friend. Someone who understood.

"See you Thursday, Maddie. It was so nice to have met you," as she waved her goodnight.

At their twice weekly meetings they soon became firm friends.

"What do you do?" asked Ursula, about six weeks later.

"I am a staff nurse in Glasgow. I love my job. And you, Ursula? Do you work?"

"Yes. I am the same. I teach primary school for my sins. I have worked there for about twelve years. And I have a daughter, Ruth, who is twenty-five. I had a son, Simon, who passed away last year. That is the reason I come to this class."

Maddie replied, "I too had a daughter, Sophie. She was six when she was taken from me. She is the reason I come to the class. Some time, I will tell you all about it, but not now."

"I fully understand, Maddie. The hatred, the nightmares, wanting to do more, but can't."

Maddie looked at Ursula with a strange expression on her face.

"Ursula," she said, "do you ever want to do harm to the person who did this to you?"

"You are telling me I do," Ursula said, but we will discuss this when we know one another better," she answered.

It took another few weeks for them to become closer. Then they would sometimes meet for coffee on Saturday mornings. However, Ursula used this time to start her plan. She had a large notebook. I will start a master plan and reveal it to Maddie. But only when I feel the time is right, not before, she thought.

For the first time in weeks, she slept soundly that night.

Chapter 8

Ursula sat mulling over how the hell it had all come to this? The doorbell rang. It was James.

"Come in and take a seat," she asked, glad of the distraction. "Would you like a coffee?"

"That would be nice," he replied. "I hope you are feeling a little better, Ursula?"

Polite as always, she thought.

"I have come about the headstone for Simon. This is the brochure." He handed a glossy book over. "You choose the stone and what you would like written on it."

"That is kind," she replied. "If you leave it there, I'll get back to you. How are Liz and Leah?" She smiled. "Have you lost weight James, are you okay?"

"They are fine and so am I. It's been a distressing time for us all. The shock, losing Simon. When the police arrived at the house, I thought they had made a mistake. I had only spoken to Simon the day before. Besides, they had pictures." He rubbed his hand over his eyes as if he was trying to rub out the memory.

"When did they visit? Pictures, what pictures?" she asked, puzzled. This was all news to her. Slowly, it dawned on her what the pictures were. Hell!

"The day after Simon died," he replied.

"With pictures," she stammered, repeating herself.

James nodded, too choked to answer.

"When they were here, much to my shame I did not ask the how and where it happened. To be honest, I was dumbstruck, my brain froze. Like you, I thought they had made a mistake."

"That's what makes it all so difficult. To be killed on a pedestrian crossing. While that man roared off. Besides, people saw it happen. Someone took his number and phoned the police. Two girls were treated for shock," he replied.

He put his head in his hands, afraid to look at her. She gave him a blank look. She could not speak. Anger rising to her throat, almost choking her.

"Are you telling me," she said as she found her voice, "that black-hearted bastard left my child lying in the road like an animal? Like some kind of roadkill," she sputtered out at last.

"Ursula, calm down. I should never have told you about the pictures. Please," he begged, "you'll do yourself harm."

"You did right to tell me. What did I get? The sanitised version?" she whimpered.

Later, when James had left, she thought, do men really understand what it is, to carry a child inside your body, from one tiny cell to a full-grown human being? You invest all your hopes and dreams in that child. She asked herself, do they?

Chapter 9

Saturday morning, Ursula went for a walk in Alexandra Park. To clear her mind of last night's black dreams. Remembering tightening her hands around that man's throat. Afraid to tell anyone at the class, otherwise they might think she had lost the plot, put me away. James's visit had left her beside herself with a mixture of grief, hatred and revenge. She could not sit in peace, when she stood, found herself pacing up and down. Like a caged tiger. Is this the way sane people carried on, she mused. No, no, no. This is not me, calm, sensible Ursula. *Think positive thoughts*, the lady at the bereavement class had advised. For Pete's sake, she scolded herself. Don't get mad, get even! Somehow, I don't think that's what the lady meant, she thought.

She had met two nice ladies at that class, Maddie and Glenda. I will cultivate their friendship. Seeming to family and friends to be getting on with my life. She could hardly believe what she was contemplating. Would I dare? More important, the need to get away with it.

He would be getting on with his life. Sitting in the pub. Thinking he was high and dry. He had got away with murder. Dream on, Mr Matt Thomson, dream on. Finding a journal, determined to put her plan into action, she gave it a title.

"Aftermath."

She smiled.

Chapter 10

Matt Thomson was well pissed-off. The months after the court case were hell. The Daily Record's account was bad enough. As near as dammit calling him a murderer. That was way out of him. Susan, his wife, hardly acknowledged him, let alone spoke. Bitch. Her silence said it all. Granted, they had lost a lot of friends. No invitations, not even to this year's sixties dance. In her mind, she was being punished for something she didn't do. In addition, she had warned him, not once but twice. Interfering bitch.

Thank goodness his son and family were in Australia, no hassle from them. Nosey bugger was planning a trip to see the grandkids. More likely to get away from him. She would soon fill them in, giving the story arms and legs, nae doubt. Hope she never comes back. It is all her fault for phoning the fucking polis. Bet when she comes back I'll find myself in the divorce court, toute suite, I will. Bugger. Her bloody old hag of a mother has not been around of late. Knowing her, she won't say much but think plenty. Old bitch, she won't like her respectable daughter being caught up in the fallout from this mess.

Yet, it's not as bad as it could be. My job as an off-shore worker means I'm out of the way a lot of the time. Plus, I don't need to drive, he sneered.

Everybody knew of him now. Once, twice, but three times was way over the top in most people's eyes. Shit! A guy had died. Even the blokes in his local did their best to avoid him now. It was 'Hi Matt,' from a distance before the sharp exit. Maybe he could get a job in Saudi? Dream on Tommy, with my record, forget it. Bugger them all, I'm off to the club.

Chapter 11

Glenda met her friend Cathie in Glasgow where they had both been shopping.

"It's so nice to see you again, Glenda. How are you getting along? Got time for a coffee? I'm parched," she asked.

"Always," replied Glenda. "How about some lunch?"

"Good thinking," Cathie replied. "For once, I have time as it's my day off."

"I heard you were engaged. I am so pleased for you," Glenda added.

"I met Roy at work. As you know I'm still in the travel agency. So we have similar interests. Also, some great holidays," she answered happily.

As they sat down at a cosy corner table, she went on.

"I heard you have left Ian, is that right? To be honest, it was the best news I've heard in years. Now you can get on with your own life."

"You heard right. As you know, he could not keep either his eyes or his hands to himself as far as other women were concerned. I could always be sure of his whereabouts. The pub, the snooker or football, he thought he was a single guy. Jack the lad," she laughed. "The last big bust up, I'd had enough. I told him to bugger off to one of his ladies. Much to my surprise, he did." They both laughed out loud.

The waitress took their order as they sat back to catch up.

"Luckily, I got the house. My three sisters helped me and Mum moved in. We were fine for a while at least."

"I also heard you lost your son, Glenda. When was that?"

Glenda looked up. "Sadly, about a year-and-a-half ago. I am still going to the bereavement class in town. To be honest, I can't seem to get over losing Ryan. Each day is a fight. I don't know how I would cope if I didn't have Kim, who is eight, to keep me steady."

At that point, their meal came.

"I love fish and chips," said Cathie. "Do you?" Changing the subject to a brighter note.

Glenda replied, "I don't have it too often, so it is a treat."

"Where are you working now, Glenda?" she continued.

"I am working as a carer in the Springburn district. I love it," she enthused. "Most of my clients are really nice. You would be amazed at their backgrounds. Their war stories are wonderful. Some have held great jobs."

Cathie could imagine Glenda being popular. Her pleasant personality and plump, motherly figure would be an asset as a carer, she thought. However, Cathie could sense an underlying sadness which had never been there before. Losing her little boy must have been traumatic. She would not mention it again as Glenda seemed happy for the moment.

As they parted for their separate buses, they hugged goodbye. Promising to catch up again. That was so nice, she thought, I have not laughed since I lost Ryan.

Chapter 12

Ursula sat beside Glenda at the next meeting. Maddie wasn't there.

"Ursula, she's a staff nurse and works shifts so she can't always come to the class."

Glenda looked tired and drained as if she had been crying all night.

Taking her arm as they left, Ursula suggested, "Why don't I take you for a coffee and cake. I don't think this is one of your better days? I know how you feel, I'm the same. On the other hand, I promised my daughter, Ruth, I would try harder not to let myself go. Hair done once a week, yet some days I could have pulled it all out. Make-up on each day, try and keep up, make an effort." She could have wept for Glenda, so lost. "Maybe if we told each other our stories, it might help?"

"Yes," Glenda whispered. "I can't say too much at home as my poor mum is devastated and Kim can't understand."

"Enjoy your tea, then tell me what happened. Maybe it will help," said Ursula kindly.

"My kids, Ryan and Kim, were at Bobby's birthday party," she stammered. "They were playing on the trampoline. Lots of laughter and squeals of delight while my sister, Jane, and I had tea with the other mums. Suddenly, there was silence. We all went outside to see what was wrong.

"*'Ryan fell off,'* they all said at once.

'I'm fine, Mum, just banged my head,' he said.

But Jane was wiser than me. *'Safer to have him checked over. It's no bother taking him to Accident and Emergency. Better safe than sorry.'*

"Sarah took Kim home while we went to the hospital. The wee friendly nurse made a fuss of him.

"*'The doctor will be here before long,'* she reassured us, with big smiles to make him feel better.

"A young lady doctor arrived, no smiles from her. She looked into his eyes. Tapped his knees. Listened to his heart, and pronounced, *'He's fine, just a bump, you might give him a paracetamol before bedtime,'* she said, leaving.

"*'Remember Granny used to give us syrup of figs when we fell,'* said Jane. *'That young doc was a bit brash to be dealing with children. Was she in a hurry or something? One out of twenty for bedside manner,'* she retorted.

"When we got home, Ursula, he was a little tired, maybe a bit of a temperature. So I gave him a paracetamol, a hot drink. Tucked him up on the couch. *'Bedtime.'* I put him to bed and kissed him goodnight.

"About five, I went to check on him. He was very, very hot and sleepy. I phoned Jane. *'Phone an ambulance, Glenda, I will be with you in two minutes,'* panic making her voice sound queer.

"This time it was a Sister who seen him. There was an older doctor. He asked a few questions then asked the nurse, *'Where are the X-rays from yesterday, Nurse?'*

"We told him, Ursula, he didn't get one. He said, *'He must have done as all head injuries go to X-Ray department.'* I told him he did not. The young doctor said he would be fine and sent us home. He told the nurse to get him to X-Ray department and to stay with him. Ursula, we were scared. He patted my hand. *'Not to worry, we'll soon get it sorted out.'*

"Ryan was admitted to the intensive care unit. The doctor came back with the sister. I will never forget those words:

"*'Mrs Carr, I'm afraid Ryan has a small hairline fracture of the skull. Combined with quite a bit of swelling of the brain. We will do all we can to reduce that.'*

"When we went to his bed, oh, Ursula! He was all wires and bottles and a plastic thing in his mouth. They tried to explain but I did not hear them."

Glenda started to sob. Ursula held her in her arms.

"Jane and I sat there for the next two days. He was very pale, with no sound at all. Jane, Kim and my sisters were there and Ian, his dad. My sisters came and went, taking Kim with them. Those nurses were so kind to us. Ryan held on for two days. He passed away that night. I will never get over it, Ursula. He was six.

"We were later informed that, had he been X-rayed earlier, it would have helped. The young locum, Allison Shepherd, had only been qualified for three months.

"Sarah, my sister, would not be put off. She said, *'I want an enquiry into this mess.'* I remember her hands were clenched white with temper. Allison Shepherd was given a severe reprimand. Suspended for some time. I think three months. The notice in A and E now reads: *All head injuries must be sent to the X-Ray department.*

"Ursula, please, please don't tell me to get over it. Because I can't," she pleaded.

Chapter 13

Sleep evaded Ursula. In her mind, Glenda's story replayed over and over. What she must have suffered, poor thing. Slowly watching her child dying, that was more than a young mother could bear. Ursula had been aghast just listening. I would hate to think what Glenda and her family went through. Six-years-old. That was the age group she had taught. Picturing the smiles and laughs. Their little hands in hers. The whole world at their feet, wee darlings.

Don't think of that doctor, selfish bitch, it will start my black dreams again. I might be wise to take Glenda under my wing. And I tremble to think what has happened to Maddie. She is a quite different kettle of fish, she thought as, at last, she drifted off to sleep.

Looking from their daughter, Sophie's bedroom window, Maddie Price allowed the memories to drift slowly back. It had become a habit, one she couldn't break. Sophie at a day old, a year, first tooth, first step, all those happy smiles. As she had looked at her, she could hardly believe her luck in having such a happy child. Sophie was such fun to be around. Some days it had been hard to go to work and leave her. For five years she had been the light of Maddie's life. God, had it been two years already?

The week before she had been killed, they had gone to Pizza Hut in town for lunch. Sophie could hardly eat her ice-cream for excitement. She couldn't take her bright eyes from the other children as her blond curls bounced on her restless shoulders. She was more like her father, Mark Nesbitt, who was fairer than Maddie, who had dark hair and deep brown eyes. Handsome bloody Harry, mark paid for her but there was no way he was any kind of a father. God, he had made a bloody sharp exit. Maddie could still feel her tiny hand in hers as she skipped towards the cinema.

If only she could stop the action replay going on in her head. Breathless sobs caught in her throat as she recalled that awful day. First the two police officers appearing on the ward, asking for her. Then telling her of an accident near the school gates. She could feel her throat almost closing in fear and panic. Don't tell me any more, please, she thought, but they went on.

Her Sophie was dead. In addition, her mother, who had been holding Sophie's hand, had been taken to the Royal Infirmary with a broken arm and leg.

Maddie looked at them with a blank stare. Irrationally, she wanted to punch them. They guided her towards a side room. She could see the other nurses hurrying towards her, their hands at their mouths in disbelief. She remembered feeling sorry for the policeman. As a nurse herself, she knew the script, having done this kind of thing so often herself. In her overactive mind, she could see her little one on a cold, grey pavement, her small body broken.

Only later did she learn that the man had been drunk. Bastard! She could not believe it. How the hell did the police let him get away with killing her child? Bastard! Don't tell me eighteen months in prison banned from driving and having to re-sit his test was a punishment for her Sophie. How was it possible to reduce a charge from death by dangerous driving to one of careless driving with no mention of Sophie? She was left to serve a life sentence without her daughter. She could feel the ever-present hatred rising inside her, almost swallowing her. She was the one who would have to watch Sophie's wee friends growing up, maybe going to Uni, holidays with the crowd. Getting married and being bridesmaids to each other, having fun – Maddie would not be part of all that, her life would be empty. The nights were the worst. She would awaken, dreaming of tearing his face off with her nails. These were black and dangerous thoughts. She knew she desperately needed help if she were to avoid going mad. Hatred was beginning to rule her life. She felt rather than heard her mother opening the door.

"I knew I would find you here, Maddie. You can't go on like this, we must get some help. Maybe if we asked Dr McMillan, he might be able to advise us where to go, eh Maddie?" She held Maddie in her arms. She had lost her granddaughter and now she was losing her girl too.

"Mum, I've been to bereavement counselling, it helped for a while. The six sessions distracted me but unless they can bring Sophie back, they are useless. I don't want sympathy. I will work my way through this. Also, I've been online looking at the American website, *M.A.D.D.*, *Mothers Against Drunk Driving*. But it seems to me to be mothers against drunk organisations instead of anti-drunk drivers."

Her mother listened with sadness, yet it was beyond her understanding.

Maddie went on, "It would give you a severe case of depression just looking at them. In this country all they do is publicise the parents' plight. So justice has no part of this equation."

Mrs Price asked, "Maddie, surely the police can help?"

"Mum, the police cannot help. They can only obey the law. They have no teeth and remember, they are up against extremely powerful people. I went online and seen for myself the adverts to get you off. Yes, indeed, but for ten or fifteen thousand pounds. Lawyers see these guys as real money spinners. A chance to show off their despicable skills, so to speak." Loathsome people, she almost spat out. "My child, and many like her, are the losers. Don't start me, Mum," she stormed. Maddie only wanted to kill that bastard, James Know, with her bare hands. He had taken everything good in her life. I only want revenge, hot or cold, it did not matter, she mused.

Mrs Price left quietly, closing the bedroom door.

Chapter 14

At the next meeting, Maddie looked done in.

"How are you, Maddie?" said a concerned Ursula.

"Can I have a wee word with you after the meeting, Ursula?" she replied.

"Of course you can," Ursula replied kindly.

Glenda had to go home so that meant they could go for a coffee.

"What is the problem, Maddie?" Ursula asked.

As they sat down, Maddie's face crumpled, while hot tears ran down her cheeks. Ursula felt dreadful as it was her fault for opening the floodgates.

"I can't go on like this," she sobbed. "If it wasn't for my mother being left alone, I would throw myself into the Clyde," she continued.

Opening a packet of tissues and handing them to Maddie, who mopped her face.

"No," reasoned Ursula, "you mustn't even think like that, it will solve nothing. Maybe if you tell me what the trouble is, I could help."

By the time Maddie told her story, she seemed a little calmer.

"I have been to bereavement counselling for the last year, and heaven help them, they are kindness itself. Their advice is to think and do new things and not to dwell on Sophie. They don't understand. I can't do that, not for a minute." She sniffed, taking a gulp of her drink. "My mind is full of dark thoughts, hatred and revenge. God help me, Ursula, I just want to kill him with my bare hands. I am afraid for my sanity, I really am." She had stopped sobbing by now but was still very upset.

Ursula understood, oh yes. Oh yes, she understood perfectly.

Maddie, you and I are kindred spirits. My only son, Simon, was killed a while ago by a drunk driver who then got off scot-free. A clever lawyer, Campbell McIntosh, got him off. I think the best way for you and I to proceed is to look at solutions, not problems. We must forget feeling sorry for ourselves. Just like Mr McIntosh, we need a plan of action that will work. We need to ensure that justice is done.

"I want you to go home. Spend the week sorting yourself out, as I will do. I am working on something that might help us. I also think that Glenda might join us in our project. What do you think?"

"She is heartbroken, Ursula, beyond anything I have seen but I think she will join our wee group."

As they both left for home, they could both see a tiny light at the end of the tunnel.

Chapter 15

"Well, well," Ursula said out loud. "Just when I thought things could not get any worse, a small glimmer of hope appears on the horizon. I'm talking to myself now, what next?"

She could see that Maddie and Glenda had been badly treated. Like her, wanted to repay someone for their hurts.

She had an idea of where to proceed from here and her heart was racing with anticipation. An extremely busy weekend lay ahead. Knowing what you wanted and achieving it were two very different things. Firstly, she needed a plan or at least an outline of one. It would need meticulous organisation if they were to succeed. Her first major hurdle would be selling it to Maddie and Glenda. Then to convince them they were capable of doing it. Glenda might be a problem. Truth to tell, it was no small thing to take someone's life.

I will have to weld them, using their combined hatred, sense of abandonment and need for revenge into a tight, unbreakable circle.

George Square in Glasgow city centre is much loved by its citizens, to whom it is simply known as *'The Square'*. Home to the Glasgow City Council, which opened in 1888. It has an impressive collection of statues of the great and the good. The square is always busy with workers sitting on the many memorial benches, eating lunch, elderly people feeding the pigeons or just resting. Or just enjoying that infinite pastime: people watching.

Ursula sat in the sun, warming her face. Closing her eyes, she could hear the laughter of children who were chasing the birds. They would never catch them, those pigeons were streetwise.

Her peaceful exterior was at odds with her mind, full of dark and dangerous thoughts. Pull yourself together, she rebuked herself.

Maddie, Glenda and Ursula had become firm friends, going for coffee after the meetings each week. Ursula had invited them to lunch in Browns Restaurant in the square. Only saying she had something important to discuss with them.

Chapter 16

Ursula drove into the city centre the following Saturday to meet Glenda and Maddie. She was suddenly overwhelmed with apprehension. Both her head and tummy were turning cartwheels. Before leaving the house, she had given herself a final once-over. The cream trouser suit had been a good choice.

Annette, her hairdresser, had given her a wee lift, saying, "How about some blonde highlights for a wee change, Ursula, make you feel better?"

She had a decent figure and always dressed well.

"Yes," she agreed.

She was aware of the importance of this meeting, their whole lives would change forever. Questions raced around her mind. Could they make a team? Will we be able to pull it off? More important, would they get caught? Not if I have anything to do with it.

Place your smile on. This is for Simon, she told herself for the tenth time today. Sitting on a bench, her mouth and her knees turned to jelly. She saw the ladies. Maddie, capable and efficient, while Glenda, capable in her own way, was slightly plump, a motherly-looking girl. I pray this enterprise doesn't change her too much. Ursula knew fine well it would.

She greeted them with a smile.

"Hello ladies, nice to see you both. Before we go to Brown's for lunch, take a note of the name on this memorial bench as we may have to use it for a couple of weeks," she added.

"Duncan Anderson," Maddie replied, reading the inscription. "He sounds nice," she added.

Ursula explained. "There are CCTV cameras all over the square. We three have suddenly become camera shy, we leave here one at a time," adding, "see you over there ladies."

They settled into a nice out-of-the-way table. Looking around, Glenda said, "This is nice, Ursula," while Maddie nodded.

The waiter took their order then brought three sparkling waters, which they sipped.

Ursula continued, "I'm going to lay out my plan, so listen carefully. We must all agree. If anyone disagrees, they are free to leave. Is that clear? I will explain. We have all lost our children. I would go so far as to say, murdered by people who got away with it." She looked at them, taking another sip of her water.

"The justice system has jump-started any action we take. Therefore, they cannot complain when we play them at their own game," she declared. "The police do all they can however, they must work within the law. Criminals, who pay lip service to the law. Lawyers, who see the law as some kind of a game. The money they make is beyond belief. They flaunt the law in a casual manner," she argued. "They will have to learn there is a price to be paid. It's called justice. We will show them justice, true justice. We three will be judge and jury." She smiled like some old, sinister gangster. She paused for breath, taking a long drink before continuing.

"The plan for this undertaking will be as if for WW3, organised down to the last detail. These detestable people have overlooked one tiny detail. Criminals and lawyers who defend them all work extremely hard at their careers. Our children are our life's work, not a job. How much harder will we work to avenge our children?" she questioned.

At that, their meal arrived, looking delicious as always in Brown's. Ursula noticed that Glenda had stopped twisting her hands.

"Just relax and enjoy your meal," she urged.

She could sense the doubt between them. It would be up to her to convince them to join together and eliminate this trash. The emphasis being on their own peace of mind when it was done. You will have to box clever here, she mused to herself.

Coffee arrived and they both looked a bit more relaxed.

"I do realise what I am proposing ladies, and understand it is a lot to take in. Why don't we meet on the bench at one o'clock next Saturday? Have a good hard think, make your decision and we'll take it from there," Ursula said.

She could not be fairer than that.

Chapter 17

Maddie could not sit still, pacing up and down like a wild animal. She had cleaned the already neat wee house till it gleamed. She would tread a hole in the carpet next. Her mother had gone to her friend's so would be another couple of hours. Her mum's last word as she left, "Maddie, goodness sake, you're like a hen on a hot griddle, sit down."

Get your act together girl, she told herself.

She tried lying on the couch trying to unscramble her thoughts. Ursula had seriously been suggesting they kill these three people. She could hardly absorb this. Had she got it right?

I cannot believe it. If I am honest with myself, I have been dreaming for the last year about doing him in, wee rat. Could they really pull it off? It just might be the right time to pay these bastards back. Ursula has a plan. She will be the one in charge. I think I will say yes on Saturday. Now her mind was made up, she felt better. I'm fed up with nightmares, racing heart, stomach in a whirl, can't eat for temper.

Her mum would notice the change, she never missed a trick. Some story would have to be concocted about feeling better. That part is true, if he was going to pay. I will feel ever so much better.

Maddie met Glenda in the tearoom in Stobhill on Thursday. A cheery place full of busy people.

"Hi Glenda," she called over. "Have you got time for a cuppa?"

"I have. I've just seen my client home."

Settling down to their tea and biscuits, Glenda murmured, "I'm so ready for this cuppa. I seem to get more down by the day, Maddie."

"I want to talk about Ursula's plan," Maddie blurted out. "It has been on my mind night and day, puzzling over it till my head is nipping."

"I'm too much of a coward to do it, Maddie. And I haven't got the brains. I would get caught," she lamented.

"Glenda, stop getting all hot and bothered." She could see her friend was at the end of her tether. "You have the same brain as me. What we are going to do is get our act together. Are you telling me some stupid, selfish wee lassie is going to destroy you and your family? Glenda! The only way people can hurt you is if you let them. Now are you willing to join us or not?" she queried.

Glenda's trembling hands picked at the uneaten biscuit as a few stray tears slid down her cheeks.

"I made up my mind the other day. Now are you with us?" she smiled.

"Yes, Maddie," she sobbed, "I'm in anything to take this awful pain away."

God, Maddie thought, those chips smelt good.

Chapter 18

Ursula went ahead with her plans even though she was still unsure of the ladies' intentions. Grateful, at last, to have something other than reruns of Simon's funeral to think about. She was up half the night planning and scheming. On the other hand, she was slowly filling her journal, *Aftermath*. It will be up to me to solve the problem of convincing the ladies, she told herself. Maddie was much more confident than Glenda yet I think her sense of deep loss and intense hatred might be the turning point.

Saturday saw Ursula in the square on 'their' bench. This was the day all her hopes were pinned on. Yes or no?

Maddie and Glenda arrived within minutes of each other, Maddie with a determined step, Glenda a wee bit apprehensive. Ursula smiled warmly.

"Nice to see you, ladies," she said while at the same time her insides were churning and her heart hammering in her chest.

"You too, Ursula. I see you are on our bench," added Maddie.

"Yes, but I hope not for too long. I will tell you later. Why don't we go over to Brown's again and enjoy our lunch? I missed breakfast so I'm ready for something now."

Once again, they were in the restaurant having ordered, sipping their drinks. They looked at each other, each with their own solemn thoughts.

After their meal, Ursula looked at them both while they awaited coffee. They all seemed a little more relaxed, yet Maddie could feel Glenda's knees trembling under the table. She gave her an encouraging smile as she laid her hand on hers.

"I know it's been a dreadful week for you both. We have all been wracked by indecision. It is a lot to take in. First, I need your answers. Maddie, are you willing to join us, yes or no?" said Ursula.

Maddie answered in a firm voice, "Yes, Ursula, I am."

"Glenda, what about you?" inquired Ursula.

"I was really afraid at first thinking more of getting caught. What about Mum and Kim? A lot of thought told me it was the only thing to do. It is the only peace I am ever going to get. I must be a nightmare to my family to live with as I am. So yes, Ursula, I'm in," she replied with a smile.

"Well done, ladies, we are now a team. And we will solve this dilemma, one, by looking at solutions, not problems, and two, by pulling together and helping each other. We must be closer than family, almost welded together," she said as she sipped her coffee.

They each had tears in their eyes as they surveyed one another.

"I have been laying out a plan for the last two weeks. I'm waiting word for a small rented flat at George Cross as we cannot meet here too often with all these cameras.

"This flat is for my niece who is down from Inverness doing a course at university and is rented in her name, Cathleen McLaren. Simon left quite a bit of money so we have no worries on that score. Any questions so far?"

"Will your niece not wonder what we are doing in her flat, Ursula?" asked Glenda worriedly.

"Well, I've not actually got a niece," she said with a sly smile. "Any more questions?"

"No," they both said breathlessly, as if they could hardly believe what they were hearing.

"The flat is ours for a year. It will be our headquarters. Outside of it, we cannot be seen together or phone or email each other. So here are some bits and bobs you will need."

At that she opened her large handbag, removing two boxes.

"These are your new mobile phones. We only use them to call each other and we will have a new sim card every month. Get rid of the old one away from home. Also, these envelopes contain five hundred pounds. Do not put it in the bank. You will need cash to do your shopping. Do this a little at a time. More is not a problem, just ask. I know it's a lot to take in but it's for your own safety.

"It would be simple to drop a little atropine into their tonic water which the police would suss out in five minutes. Another thing, we are not capable of any kind of violence. We must be extremely careful leaving no evidence. For this enterprise it is brains not brawn," she contended.

"I will be at our new flat from next week as I will be off work sick."

They both looked at her quizzically.

"I am sick, heartily sick of people making a clown of me," she retorted.

As the bill arrived, they were all deep in thought. Shit, mused Maddie, she has not missed a trick. I'll bet she has a plan all laid out. Crumbs!

"One last thing. . . Tell mums and sisters we are going to our bereavement counselling twice a week. Because you are feeling the better for it. You *are* both going to feel a whole lot better as this is the start of your new vocation. As with any new career, there is a lot to learn. For example, lying, cheating, acting, dressing up and learning your lines. Ladies, we just might enjoy some aspects of our new employment," she added cheerfully. "It's called retaliation."

"Ursula, do you really think we three are up to all this?" Maddie asked.

Before Ursula could reply, Glenda blurted out, "Of course we are, Maddie, it's an eye for an eye time, we are just paying them back."

Both Ursula and Maddie looked at one another with a look that said, *Oh dear, I think we have awakened a sleeping tiger.*

See you next week, ladies, remember it's our last week on our bench. Bye now."

They left the restaurant one by one.

Chapter 19

Ursula had an extremely busy week. The flat in George Cross was just off the motorway. Handy for all, it had a small lounge, two bedrooms, kitchen and bathroom. A few sticks of furniture, seemingly called *'partly furnished for students'*. The agent did not even blush as she signed the lease for a year.

She then embarked on a merry-go-round of shopping. A bit of luck with the seating: a shop in Great Western Road was having a sale.

As she entered, a nice young man inquired, "Can I help you, Madam?"

"I have a bit of a problem," explained Ursula. "My niece is coming to Glasgow to do a course at university. We need seating for her and two friends who will occasionally share with her. However, we need them as soon as possible."

At that, Ursula took a bundle of cash from her handbag. She had been given this tip by a lady in sales. Once they had seen the cash, it would help them to solve her problem. These young men lived by commission, so this was a gift. He was more than helpful.

"Well, Madam, we don't have many chairs in stock but luckily we have three matching recliner chairs in the stockroom and could deliver at your convenience. Cream leather."

"That would be really good," she replied. "Do you think you could also help me to pick out three cheerful rugs as well?"

"Not a bother, Madam, we have a rather nice selection in-store."

When she had chosen three rugs, he escorted her to the payment desk.

"Thank you so much, young man. I'll pay cash. My name is Sinclair, Jean Sinclair. Also, the name on the flat is McLaren, for the delivery man." Politely giving a lady at the desk her cash and details.

Then it was off to the supermarket for kitchen equipment, such as a kettle, toaster, microwave and dinner set. Three duvets just in case of sleepovers. Nothing could be brought in from their homes. Every single item must be new. Plastic storage boxes were a must. She put them on her next shopping list.

Good job done, she told herself. She almost danced down the street. Now back to the flat. Things were shaping up nicely. They were nearly there as far as the flat went. I'll see the girls on Saturday, she thought, I can hardly wait. Feeling better, it is so long since I've felt anything but miserable. Wonderful what having a goal can do.

Tomorrow, it would be bank, keys cut, and groceries. Also, three small handbags for our essentials, phone, keys and cash and two large storage boxes with drawers for keeping our plunder.

She loved being busy.

Chapter 20

Saturday dawned bright with a gentle breeze. Ursula turned her face up to enjoy it while waiting. The ladies appeared within five minutes of each other, greeting each other warmly and taking a seat on their bench.

"No need to go to Browns today as the flat is more or less ready. I'm parked around the corner so follow me to our wee flat, it's on the first floor. There we can discuss our next move over lunch," explained Ursula.

Putting the kettle on as she set the small kitchen table with a light lunch.

Glenda was first then Maddie.

"This is lovely," proclaimed Maddie looking around, all smiles.

"These seats are beautiful, every home comfort. Many a student would love this plus you could rent it out when we are finished."

"Maybe I will," agreed Ursula. "Now I have a nice quiche for lunch and a wee treat of strawberry tarts. Have a seat. Would you like tea or coffee?"

"Coffee please, I can't believe this place. It has everything we need. I could move in no bother," she added with a laugh.

They seemed like three different people almost as if they had been given a new lease of life. After lunch they settled in their seats.

Glenda exclaimed, "Oh my, these are recliner seats. I have always wanted one of these," as she settled back into the chair.

"Now you have one," joked Ursula. "Right, down to business," she said seriously.

"Next week you both have quite a bit to do so make out your lists. When you have the items on it, destroy it. We can't have anything on us that can be used against us, real names or phone numbers. I have these small leather handbags for keys, cash and phones. Also, I have put one thousand pounds in the drawer in your bedrooms. Use as and when needed."

They both went to protest but putting up her hand, she said, "You will need it, ladies." She paused and went on. "I have worked out a job rota for us. If there is anything you want to add, feel free to do so. I will be in charge of planning, alibis and cash. We will each need to be away on holiday while our individual business is being done. I will take care of that side of things. If you want to take your mothers or sisters just say so, it is no great problem. Also stocking up the flat. We will need more of those storage boxes for all this stuff.

"Maddie, you will oversee all the drugs with researching, buying and instructing Glenda and me in their use. We will all work together on transport. By the way, I've parked Simon's car outside the flat. You will have to come up with your own lies for that. Maybe my niece's fellow students, use it now and then. I will sort out the paperwork.

She gave a sigh. "A wee cup of tea might be helpful now?"

Maddie nodded, leaving for the kitchen.

As they drank their tea, Ursula continued. "Glenda, you will be our wardrobe mistress. You will need an assortment of things such as wigs in different colours and styles. I'll leave that up to you. Hoodies, dark tracksuits, also trainers and leather gloves. We will need those all-in-one white decorating suits from B&M. I advise getting six, you never know. In addition, gloves, get leather. I was reading a guidebook for writers by a real CSI, Kate Bendelow, very useful for our enterprise. She advises using leather as they can get fingerprints from other kinds. Everything must be kept here, nothing at home. We will all take turns at being taxi drivers as quite a lot of tailing will be important. We will need to get false number plates though, where you get them, I have not a clue."

Glenda said, "Ursula, we might need boot bags for each car and seat covers with snacks, drinks, torches and jump leads. Including Simon's car."

"Good thinking, Glenda," said Maddie.

"I hope we have covered just about all we need just now. Glenda and I will do all the shopping. You, Maddie, will have more to think about. You will have to read up on the drug scene." She rubbed her hands together. "Well," she said, "it's been a busy day for us all. Remember we meet here next Saturday about twelve-thirty and catch up."

They left one by one.

Chapter 21

Glenda had a grand time. She had become a professional shopper as well as a habitual liar.

First, she went to the wig shop in Glasgow where cancer patients went. A young woman came towards her.

"Can I help?" she asked pleasantly.

"My name is Mrs Moore. I am a carer and need to buy a few wigs for my clients," she explained to the girl.

"No bother, Madam. Pleased to help."

"I have a list here. One will have to be grey and short as Mrs Green is elderly. That is about all she can manage."

The girl came back with a nice grey wig. Might do Maddie or me if we are cleaners, Glenda thought.

"Also, two fair ones, something nice for about my age, one a short bob, the other a little longer. And a shoulder-length bob would be nice for Alice and can I have a dark-brown one for Eve? I think I might take another grey. A bob will do fine for Betty," she said politely. The young lady sat in front of a mirror, turning each one in turn to let Glenda see for herself.

"They are very nice. I'll take them all." She smiled as the lies slipped from her tongue.

"How would you like to pay, Mrs Moore?"

"I'll pay cash, dear, thank you so much for all your help."

She left the shop with her six wigs in fancy bags. "Great," she said to herself. She put the bags in the boot and then went to Primark where she acquired three large bags of plunder.

When Glenda arrived at the flat on Saturday, Ursula had the kettle on the boil.

"Come on in, Glenda, nice to see you. My, you've been a busy bee this week by the look of those bags."

Ursula poured the tea, placing chicken sandwiches on the small table. They sat in their respective seats. Both had large notebooks stuffed down the side.

"How did you manage this week?" asked Ursula.

"Not too badly. I bought cheap trainers. Two fours and a five, and instead of tracksuits, I got waterproof trousers and tops plus dark scarves.

"At the wig shop, I bought six wigs, for my recovering cancer clients, you know. . . two fair – different styles – one auburn bob, one dark, a little more stylish, and two grey, one a short bob, the other a longer bob. I thought if we need to be cleaning ladies they might be more suitable. Then I remembered overalls, so they are on the list. The young lady was nice enough to model them for me."

Sipping her tea and munching a sandwich, she went on.

"I got the leather gloves in Primark, cheap as chips, Ursula. Also, two sets of plastic storage boxes as we are filling up fast," she explained.

At that, the door opened and Maddie entered.

"Sorry to be late, ladies. I met a girl who had some interesting information. Is that tea and sandwiches? Oh, I'm ready for these."

While she had her tea, Ursula went on. "The next thing we have to do is a bit of sleuthing. I've found out where the two men live. Matt Thomson, with his wife in Knightswood, James Knox, with his folks in Springburn and, Allison Shepherd, a flat in Lenzie, with two other girls. All three are dependent on public transport or lifts from friends.

"Oh, what a shame," commiserated Glenda. "So sorry, that was naughty. Couldn't help myself."

"They are all working. Thomson, on the rigs. He is away three weeks, then home for two. I would say that is handy. Knox has a new job with the council in the garden department. And Shepherd is still in the same hospital but a different department."

"Do they all work near to where they live?" Glenda asked.

"None too far away. We will have to follow and learn as we go along. No risks. We can't be seen by any of them," replied Ursula. "I've noticed lots of people standing outside shops and offices smoking cigarettes, or those vapour things. We will buy some. . . and a lighter. You never know when we will need that wee skill. Now, we will have a coffee break before we hear from Maddie."

Over coffee, Ursula continued. "The main thing is the order we do them in and what we can use and where. We will have to brainstorm for that. It's a case of ca'canny for us.

"Maddie is the expert on drugs and what we can get away with. James Knox is a known drug user. That might be useful. But, we will leave that just now. What have you managed this week, Maddie?"

"It's been more a thinking and planning time for me. Drugs are always a bit difficult. I estimate we will need three different kinds: heroin, cocaine, or crack, is sold on the street at twenty-five percent strength. You can get it at fifty percent at a price but you must be in the know. Heroin, you can buy in powder form, usually mixed with flour or baking powder to make it more profitable. Or, better for our purpose, in pill form which we can crush and add easily. I would be taking a great risk trying to buy in Glasgow. Seemingly, Dundee is the drugs capital in Scotland. Also, there is a big rise in the number of deaths. Word is, someone is selling a bad batch. You can never tell who I might have nursed here. So, my idea is to go to Dundee where I am not known. I could disguise myself as a working girl every weekend. I have some syringes in my bag. I need to get a feel for the place."

Glenda giggled.

"If you think you can deal with it then go ahead. But no risk-taking, Maddie," Ursula urged.

"What is worrying me is all that lying to Mum so I can be available Friday and Saturday nights for a couple of weeks. Ursula, I was hoping you could work out a wee break covering both weekends. I will be on sick leave from this Monday as I will be planning and also up to Dundee to see what the scene is up there."

"Worry no more, Maddie, I'll fix it. Has your mum a wee pal who might like to join her on a break? And one thing more, have you any idea how much drugs cost?"

"Not sure. I'll not bring attention to myself by haggling," added Maddie.

"Too right," retorted Glenda. "Some of these guys are bad."

"Now, ladies, one thing that worries me is the constant fear of being caught that will be with us all the time. No way do we want that. Check everything twice. Take care, no matter what. I'm thinking, Maddie, if there is a surge in drug-related deaths the police will be even more vigilant than normal. More of a police presence on the street and pubs and clubs. As far as I see, these people even target schools and colleges.

"Right, ladies, you have plenty to think about this week. I'll see you in two weeks, Maddie and you, Glenda, next Saturday. Bye now. Same exits as usual."

Chapter 22

The police in Glasgow were indeed having a busy time. Detective Inspector Diamond had been up to his neck in work for the last two or three weeks. There had been a great deal of interaction between two rival gangs in the city of late. More than likely over drugs. Four stabbings, two quite serious but so far, no fatalities. Of course, with these guys one could never tell. There were always fights however, things appeared to be escalating and it was only a matter of time before the first body would be found in a dark alley. It made no difference how many of his men were on the streets. It was a forgone conclusion. As long as they were busy establishing top dog it would continue. The profits in this game were too high not to try.

DI Diamond was at his desk, deep in thought. In his early forties, tall and solidly built. A widower with two grown children. He had come up through the ranks, a truly professional policeman. He did not suffer fools gladly, expecting each man and woman on his team to pull their weight. Not asking anybody to do anything he had not done or wouldn't do himself. A popular man who one could rely on. There was not much Diamond had not seen in his career and he had obviously earned his nickname 'The Rough'.

DS Andrew McNeil came in carrying a large folder. He was tall, not thin but not bulky. He was a pleasant, civil man. Thorough and fair, which made him good at his job. He could be described as a wee bit serious. At the same time, he was popular with his fellow policemen. He had worked with DI Diamond a long time which made them a good team.

"Morning, Sir, could you sign this lot for me please?"

As DI Diamond opened the folder and started signing, he asked, "How are things at your end, Andrew?"

"To be quite honest, Sir, you can almost smell the atmosphere on the streets. Something is brewing which will end in trouble. The big boys are conspicuous by their absence. Both Sullivan and Stewart are in some dark corner plotting like hell against one another while their men appear to be watching and waiting.

"I only hope it's only our local bad boys in the fray. God forbid if Manchester or London mobsters try to muscle in on the act," mused John.

"Hell, that would be trouble indeed. Our guys on the street tell me no one will speak a word. Also they say there is an element of fear amongst the dealers," Andrew continued.

"We will have to keep a careful eye on the whole situation. It's wait and see time. What about this bad batch situation? Have you heard anymore?"

"Not yet. It's not so much Glasgow but word is, Dundee is having a big drugs problem. Things are quiet on that front just now. Personally, I think the addicts are scared too. The dealers will still have some of the bad stuff in hand which they must get rid of at some point," Andrew answered.

"Oh, I agree with you there. They will offload it onto some young first timers no doubt. These guys are vicious, only caring for profit. We will need to crack down on them really hard, Andrew."

"Yes Sir," agreed Andrew.

Chapter 23

While Maddie was learning her trade in Dundee, Glenda and Ursula were learning theirs in Glasgow. They soon found out that it was a lot more difficult than it looked on television. Glenda was a bundle of nerves as she entered the scrap dealer's yard.

"Can I help you, hen?" asked the guy in the hut. He was accompanied by a huge, rather dirty dog.

"Yes, I'm looking for a wing mirror for my sister's car," she explained as she handed over a card with all the details of Simon's car on it.

"Aye, hen, just go up there and look around and we will get it for you," he replied. "There are a few in a wee pile up at the back."

She found one, plus two sets of number plates which she stuffed into her overlarge handbag. As she paid the man, she caught a glimpse of herself in a dirty old mirror. I suit that auburn wig, she told herself. As she drove home, she had to stop as her knees were knocking and she could feel the sweat trickling down her back.

Next day, she was trailing James Knox. Most mornings, he got a lift to work at the garden department in Springburn. He was in a kind of potting shed. Moving plants into boxes. Most likely for the gardeners to plant in flower beds. Surprisingly, he went swimming Tuesdays and Thursdays after work. That gave her a chance to investigate the place where the cleaning ladies kept their equipment.

Handy, she thought, you never know when I will need that little bit of information. Knox went for a pint in his local, meeting two mates. Also, she spied one pal handing over a wee white package. That's always good to know if it means the bugger is still using. He has not learned his lesson. Well, you soon will, boy.

Next two days found her catching up with the shopping. It seemed to be never-ending. However, she enjoyed it.

Glenda and Ursula met in the flat, Saturday. As they sipped their coffee, Glenda went over all her news.

"I don't think I have ever been so agitated in my life, Ursula. I was quite nauseous at times. I found tailing him difficult, I must admit. *Hard work is no easy*, as my granny used to say. How did *you* get on?"

They both chuckled.

"Same as you, Glenda. I admit these people who do it for a living are brave. I only had one week tailing Thomson and then he was away to the rigs," she said. "We now, though, have a fairer idea of what he gets up to. He is in that club every day, all day. The only other place he goes is to the Indian restaurant for dinner. Or the Chinese takeaway when his wife is not around. I have all the times written on the board under 'T'. He is as regular as clockwork." She paused.

"He doesn't go to football or bowling like most men. And I'll bet he never takes his wife anywhere, that's for sure.

"Talking about tailing, I had a piece of luck the other day. Monday, I think, when he left, I had a notion to follow her. I was sitting two seats behind Mrs Thomson in the health centre. That was scary. I was sure they would see me but my luck held, Glenda. She was talking to her friend and complaining about him, his boozing, smoking. . . and then she let slip he's a diabetic, and he injects himself. That will be a gift for Maddie. She was going on and on.

"*'His drinking is getting worse and he smokes like a chimney. I'll tell you, Sarah, I tell you, I have had enough this time.'*" Ursula attempted to mimic Thomson's wife's voice.

"Her friend just looked at her with sympathy. *'It must be very upsetting for you,'* she agreed then Mrs Thomson continued. *'What with the scandal of the drink driving. A young man lost his life over his selfish behaviour. We hardly have any friends left, no one wants to know us anymore. He is scum and that's a fact.'* Then the friend said, *'I don't think people appreciate how serious an illness it is. There are all kinds of complications.'* And Thomson's wife sniffed as she said, *'Not him, he thinks he's bloody immortal.'*

"At that, her name was called and I left." Ursula was almost breathless after reporting the conversation to Glenda.

"Well done, Ursula, Maddie will be pleased," Glenda whispered. "She will be back next week. I have missed her and I'm dying to hear all her news," Glenda continued.

At that, they both got up to leave.

Chapter 24

Drugs were Maddie's side of things and she had spent a great deal of time studying their effects. Cocaine powder is the one that produces the most profit for suppliers. It is often mixed with baking powder to produce 'rock cocaine' or 'crack' and then can be smoked. Sometimes known as 'nose candy' when it is inhaled. It does not seem to be widely known. It is far more dangerous to young people as it can cause damage to the central nervous system. Heroin or 'H' is a highly addictive drug also called 'smack' or 'snow'. Also, it is ten times more poisonous than cocaine. Death can take place within minutes if overdosed. Ecstasy, or the 'party pill' is popular with the young as it is easy to take. It is usually pink with a smiley face imprinted on it. Therefore, looks harmless.

Maddie knew a lady who had moved to Aberdeen. They were having a drink when Debbie told her laughingly, "Most of the working girls in Dundee were having boob jobs done," she said, "no doubt to boost trade, Maddie, so alteration shops were extremely busy.

"Most of these girls could get the stuff no bother as they spent a lot of time in one or two local pubs," Debbie recommended. "The Open Arms or The Old Inn. Not your kind of place, Maddie, but it's where the girls go."

Most helpful, thought Maddie to herself.

This was a 'what if' time for her. *If* she could pass herself off as a working girl and *if* she could easily pass herself off as a user. She knew all the signs then she would buy all she needed. I'll drive up there and see what's what, cameras, pubs and bed and breakfast.

There was no point in trying to steal from work. Checks were constantly being made. Wee mistakes were often made yet, as far as she was concerned, it's better this way. Ursula would keep her right and she would be home on Thursday in time for Mum's wee weekend away.

If I'm truthful with myself, I'm looking forward to it all starting. . . with a kind of awful fascination, she mused to herself.

Next day, she went for it. Life had become unreal. From being a sensible staff nurse with responsibilities to being a flighty dame who did not give a bugger about anything but outfits and make-up. Then she realised this must be the way actors feel as they read and rehearse for a new part. I can remember reading that the actor, Alec Guinness, could not get his character right until he had the walk correct. The moment she put her thigh-length red patent boots on she was her new self. It worked, she was Patsy Devine. For one naughty moment she wished that swine, Mark Nesbitt, could see her now. He would get a piece of her mind.

God, that perfume was strong. I had better remember to put a dab of whisky on a tissue, one couldn't be a tee-total working girl. Sitting in front of the mirror, gazing at her new face, thick, darker make-up, bright red lippy, false eyelashes and heavy black eyeliner. The purple eyeshadow was perfect. Hell, those eyelashes were longer than Daisy the cow's. Laughing at the gold gypsy earrings topped by a blonde wig, the ultra short skirt with a gold sequinned top and a push-up bra underneath which completed the dire ensemble.

These girls must be freezing in winter, she thought. I've almost nothing on. At least I have a wee furry jacket to hold the heat in.

"Bugger, I cannot resist it, looking at the stranger in the glass," she said. "Hello Patsy, nice to meet you," she winked.

Using her phone to take a selfie and then messaging it to the girls, she wrote,

Patsy Devine in Dundee, much love.

I hope they delete it soon, she thought. Because she was in a B and B, she had brought a long trench coat to cover the worst of her outfit.

The first couple of nights, she decided to flit from one pub to another. She felt a wee bit more at home in The Open Arms. It was a cosy kind of a place and very busy. There were quite a few women in the same mould as Patsy. They were friendly enough and after a few drinks they got around to chatting.

"Are you from around here?" said the younger one.

"No," said Patsy, "I'm here for a month visiting my old aunty who is in a care home."

"I'm Cathy Shaw," she said, "working name, Susie." A plain girl, she had thick make-up on and glitter on everything. More like camouflage. She looked as if she had been brought up in the school of hard knocks. Maddie's heart went out to her. Underneath all that muck, she was just a wee lassie. "This is Sadie, working name, Angela." They both looked as if they had been around the block a few times, thought Maddie.

"Are you up here to work, hen?" asked Sadie.

"No, no," said Patsy. "I'm up here to see my old aunty. She's in a care home. I'll be up here a month but I'm in a B and B and looking for a room to rent. Do you know anywhere?"

"I do," said Cathleen. "Next to me. Nothing much, but cheap. I could ask for you."

Maddie was wise in letting them know she only did business in Glasgow.

"I have no interest in business in Dundee, too near the court for my liking," she smiled.

These streetwise ladies soon saw she was no threat to them so became a wee bit more friendly. She learned they knew every copper in town.

"I need to get back to town tomorrow, ladies, so I'll see you all next weekend."

She could feel a tick in her neck going like a wee hammer. Time for a sharp exit.

"Shit," she said to the mirror in her room. "That was hard, way more difficult than I could have imagined."

Maddie fell into bed, shattered.

Chapter 25

The smell of newly cut grass wafted along the street from tiny front gardens. It had been years since Ursula had walked from Charing Cross. Not much had changed, still lots of students linking arms, chatting cheerfully, so happy it was Saturday. Older folk were walking at their leisure, shopping or looking in windows, some meeting friends for lunch. The West End was a great place to shop. She had previously spent many a happy hour here. I'm meeting friends for lunch, she told herself, however, on a much darker business. Walking had given her time to get things in perspective. There was a whole lot more to this venture than she had first thought. In addition, her main task was to keep her ladies safe. This was the first meeting for two weeks. A good bit to catch up on, I'm sure.

Ursula had lunch ready as the ladies arrived.

Maddie, glad to be back, sank into her chair. Glenda was beaming to see her again.

"Thank goodness that's the really hard part over. I would work all the double shifts Sister gave me rather than do what those girls do," Maddie revealed.

"Was it hard, Maddie?" queried Glenda.

"I, for one, would never condemn these girls, the punters, as they call them. That's the easy part. It's the men, the pimps, who live off them, taking up to forty percent of all their earnings. Then they have the no-good buggers they live with, who moreover, never work and never want, waiting for the cash to be handed over. No wonder they nearly all have a habit, poor sods," Maddie commented wryly.

"We loved the photo of Patsy," said Glenda. "You know how down I get, Maddie, but that cheered us up no end. We were worried sick, thinking of you with all those tough women and bad men. Right enough, you must have been scared skinny."

"You're right, Glenda," Maddie confessed.

At that Ursula brought in the coffee. As they thanked her, she went on.

"We must try and pool our information as right now it resembles a jigsaw puzzle. The first thing we must consider is what order they meet their demise and when. That lets me organise our trips. As we cannot be in this country when they are being attended to, I suggest, Maddie, you and Glenda do Thomson first while I am in New York on a four-day shopping trip. Maybe you and I will do James Knox. Maddie might like a trip to Rome. Such a magical city. Have you ever been there, Maddie?"

"No, never," Maddie replied.

"You will love it. Italians are a very down-to-earth people and the city is full of small, family-run restaurants as well as some rather spectacular sights. I might add you are welcome to take a friend. Remember, it's to help you get over your loss. The bereavement people recommended it, didn't they?"

Ursula continued, "While we are at it, Glenda you could introduce the subject of a wee holiday for your mum and Kim."

"My sisters might organise a trip. I'll drop a hint letting them think it was all their idea," Glenda replied.

Ursula looked at them both.

"Remember, ladies, you will have to work together on Thomson as I will be away. I think, as I told you on the phone, it will be helpful that he is a diabetic. Take no unnecessary risks if you can help it. Above all, you can not be seen by any of his pals or his wife. Will you do it at his club?"

Maddie replied, "I have worked on four or five different methods. Most will not work. Plan one was to give him an overdose of insulin however that would probably only make him feel better. I think plan two is better. We will need a bit of hard thinking to make it work.

How to get hold of his syringe is the big problem. I would need to empty it and refill it with water. That would work. These things come pre-filled with the correct amount. I could bring my water filled one and change it in the taxi. Glenda will be the driver. I might have to try and get into his flat and that would be dangerous. Glenda and I will work on it."

Ursula interrupted here.

"Maddie, remember his lifestyle. He goes for an Indian or Chinese. That's not good for him. They have a couple of bottles of wine with the meal. Then on to the club. I counted. He had seven pints of beer and five whiskies on Saturday night plus he smokes like a chimney. Is that any help?"

Maddie thought for a moment.

"Well, it is in a way. Diabetics take their short-acting shot in the morning and the long-acting one at night. This evening one is the one I must change. A guy like him, out wining and dining, might forget to take the mid-morning one. Without his injection, he will feel hungry and tired. He may even eat a chocolate bar, which will push his sugar levels up even further. God alone knows what all that booze and fags will do . . . I haven't worked that out yet. Glenda is my pre-booked taxi, waiting for me. Maybe I could offer him a lift home. That's my chance. I won't go into details but he will not feel too good, then go into a coma and not awaken. Remember his wife goes to her sister's most weekends, so he is home alone, no help. Most likely, she will find him on Sunday. The beauty of this plan is it does not look like murder with his lifestyle, he has caused it himself." Maddie paused to think about the plan.

"I'm not sure what happens next. She will most likely call the doctor or an ambulance. Police will be called as it is a sudden death. The doctor will sign the death certificate if it's his doctor. He will know he drinks and does not stick to his diet. However, we will have to keep a watch to see how it is handled," she finished.

"What do you think, Ursula?" asked Maddie.

"Sounds like a plan. On the other hand, make sure they cannot trace the taxi or the driver. Do we have extra plates for Simon's car, Glenda?" Ursula inquired.

"Yes we do, two extra, and taxi signs, which we will change when we are away from the flat," Glenda replied.

"Good, good. You two are working well. I'll leave you to work out the finer details. Also, I need to know when I can book my trip. It will need to be a week come next Friday. So, work around that timescale. I will be away four days, most likely spend the entire time worrying myself sick."

"I will spend Tuesday and Thursday evening at the swimming pool. My cleaning gear is ready," said Glenda. "As far as I can make out, the cleaning ladies are in from six till eight thirty, mornings. So I have given myself a wee evening shift. What I need to know is if and when I can get access to the cubicles. The rest of the week I am yours, Maddie."

"I have to be in Dundee this week working on my new friendships. Also, see if I can buy some cocaine or Heroine or even a few tabs of something. I won't be back till Sunday. Remember, I cannot take my car or Simon's, too many cameras near the station. So, it's the train for me this week," she added.

They left the flat, all deep in their own thoughts.

Chapter 26

Glenda's mother had called in twice this week.

"Are you all right, dear?" she inquired.

"I'm fine, Mum, just a wee bit busier than usual at work. Two girls are off sick so we all have to cover for them," she lied.

"Well, it's no bother for me to come over and make you and Kim's tea. To be honest, I'm a bit short of something to do. My wee house is cleaned in an hour then it's that telly. I can't concentrate the way I used to, soaps bore me. Folks sitting in pubs talking a load of rubbish or shouting and screaming abuse at each other," she sighed.

"That would be really kind. Tell you what, you come here about three-thirty, that's when Kim comes home, and have your tea with us. It's only an extra plate after all," Glenda replied.

"That would be just fine," her mum beamed happily.

"Sometimes I might be asked to cover for Avril's ladies, usually Tuesdays and Thursdays from five-thirty till six-thirty or seven," she went on.

"No bother, starting tomorrow, I'll bring a nice bit of haddock for our tea," Mrs Sinclair replied.

Glenda smiled. I think mum should wear a *happy to help badge* she thought. Back to more serious matters, that will let me do the two nights at the baths.

She met Ursula at the flat the next day.

"I'm up to date with Knox," she told Ursula. "So this week I will be at the baths and also watching the club where Thomson goes. We are more or less up to date with him, however Maddie is home on Sunday evening. We intend to go over the finer details. She is doing that side of things and the drugs. I don't know what she is doing yet but she knows better than me."

"That sounds fine, Glenda. Thomson does not go too far from home. Club, pub and restaurants. The man's blood must be ninety percent proof, I'm sure. But enough of him," she said. "While I'm away, I want to be thinking a little about Allison Shepherd. That might be a tricky one as we don't know too much about her. I will do the tailing with Maddie on her. You cannot be anywhere near her as she knows your face. I must confess, Glenda, I have been having nightmares about that lawyer."

"What lawyer?" asked Glenda.

"Campbell McIntosh," she continued.

"That evil man got Thomson off so he is as much to blame as Thomson is. When you think about it, when he helped him, he left him to kill again. Furthermore, Glenda, we all know Thomson is the kind of man who will not learn a lesson. To my mind, McIntosh only deals with clients like him. Somebody else will lose a child if that lawyer is not stopped," Ursula burst out.

Glenda could hardly think straight. Is she really going to finish the lawyer off as well? she thought.

"I'll leave you to have a think and maybe a word with Maddie when you are tailing. I know it's a lot to take in but it's on my mind," Ursula explained.

I just know she will do it, thought Glenda. I can feel it in my bones. Hope it's not one too far, Glenda reflected.

Chapter 27

Maddie arrived in Dundee by train leaving her bag in the left luggage as she wasn't too sure if Cathleen had managed to get her a room at her place. This was her third time meeting the 'ladies'. They all greeted her in a friendly manner, even moving around the table to make room for her.

"Were you seeing your aunty, Patsy?" asked Cathleen.

"Aye," replied Patsy. "She is fine. I don't think she knows what day it is and she repeats everything. She refers to every day as yesterday, yet she seems happy enough."

"I heard that place was good to their old people," said Gloria, "never been there myself but it has a good name, Patsy."

"That's nice then, makes me feel a bit better about her being there," Patsy replied.

"I got you a room at my place, I told her for the week, is that okay, Patsy?"

"Smashing," said Patsy. "I need to get down the road next week to make some cash."

At that, the two older ladies went over to another table to talk to some pals. Hell, thought Maddie, might as well go for it. Her knees were knocking and she could feel that bloody wee tick in her neck jumping again.

"Any chance of some stuff here, Cathleen? I'm getting a tiny bit pissed off with Aunty and mine is nearly done," she asked.

"Nae bother, when Joe comes in, I'll give you a knock down. Careful, he's a fly wee bugger," Cathleen answered.

"You canny be too careful, after all, he doesn't know me," said Patsy, aka Maddie.

She was as good as her word. When he appeared, Cathleen waved him over.

"My pal, Patsy, is looking to buy, Joe," she said softly.

"Whit dae you want, hen?" he asked.

"Cocaine, three baggies, H, can I have two tabs and two of E? That would be great," she answered. She gave the order as if she had been doing it for years. Right enough, she had practised in front of the mirror for an hour last night.

"Nae E the 'night, tomorrow I will. Might even have a couple of Ket if you fancy that, hen," he said.

"Aye, fine," she said. At the same time, her heart was banging against her ribs. She had never been so scared in her life.

"Nae bother, hen," sliding the stuff under the table at the same time quoting his price, a wee bit high. On the other hand, he was the one taking the chance, she thought. Like a ghost, he was out the door. Maddie could hardly believe she had done it. She, who had never done a wrong thing in her life. One more buy and it would be over. To keep things sweet, she slipped Cathleen one of the baggies.

"Have a drink, Cathleen, on me," she said, slipping her a tenner.

While Cathleen went to the bar, Maddie could feel the sweat trickling down her back. She did not know if it was with fear or relief.

Chapter 28

DS Andrew McNeil had just spent most of his week clearing up paperwork. It was a boring task which now gave him the most job satisfaction he had had for a while. He had so many loose ends needing to be tied in, now done. Thankfully, he could now start on the new stuff already piling up. He would now enquire what new assignment D.I. Diamond had for him.

John Diamond, a tall, well-built man in his forties had joined the force as a young man, working his way up through the ranks. Widowed a few years ago, he had two grown children. Extremely good at his job, he was proud of the team he had built around him.

"Good morning, Andrew, clearing up finished?" he asked.

"For a while at least," McNeil replied.

"The drug situation is looking grim at the moment. In fact, I would go so far as to suggest it is out of control. The Glasgow clubs are doing as they please. Word from above is, it must be stopped. So that will unfortunately be up to us. I thought Edinburgh was the biggest troublemaker with Glasgow a clear second. I think I'm wrong," he went on.

"Yes, sir, word from Dundee is even worse," said McNeil. "There have been three drug-related deaths there in the last six weeks, all young people. They seem to think it is a bad batch coming in from an unknown source. I hope it's not London or Manchester," he continued, looking troubled.

"I think we should concentrate on all the clubs. They are making a fortune for dealers. We can now confiscate cash, property and cars. For a change, the ball is in our court. Most of the big boys have already scarpered to Spain. Well out of the way, leaving their minions doing the dirty work who then use innocent young people to move the product. We have been asked to set up a four-man team to try and clear up this mess."

Diamond gave a heavy sigh. "That's us and Edinburgh, we may as well include someone from Dundee if we are to tackle this problem," he went on. "A week from today is our first meeting. You might try and get our local lads to put the squeeze on their informants. They could come up with something."

"Well, we all know it's the same old story. All the witnesses are deaf, dumb and blind when it comes to giving evidence against the big boys. The custom boys are doing a great job but it's the clubs we have to handle."

"Well, Andrew, thanks we have plenty to think about this week so good luck."

"Thank you, sir," said McNeil as he left.

Chapter 29

When Maddie and Cathleen arrived at The Open Arms the following evening, it was more than usually busy, lots of young folk. The ladies had kept them a seat, waving them over.

"Come on you two, hurry up," called Angela.

As they sat down, Cathleen asked, "What's on the night? I've never seen this place so busy."

"They're having a karaoke night and serving snacks, burgers and things," she replied.

Maddie glanced around. How could anybody eat here? The smokers left the doors open and the reek wafted in. She had to admit though, the place was spotlessly clean. The glasses sparkled while tabletops were wiped clean. Also, the waiters and barmen all had nice clean uniforms. So that said a lot.

The music was loud but catchy. Angela and Gloria both grinned.

"You know, Patsy, there are some smashing singers here."

"This is great," said Gloria. "I wish they had this every week," as she swayed from side to side.

The crowd were enjoying every minute. There was a completely different atmosphere.

"Cathleen, you get up, hen, you're a great wee singer, come on now," said Angie encouragingly.

Cathleen needed no persuading. Maddie had never seen her so happy.

"I'll tell you, Patsy, she is really good, you know, she could sing in the clubs, nae bother," Angie went on.

The audience loved her, stamping their feet for more. She obliged by giving them Gloria Gaynor's *I will survive.* She came back to the table amid much back slapping.

"You were great, hen," they called.

Maddie had to admit she was extremely good. I'm going to have a word in her ear before I leave, she mused. At that, Joe appeared, sitting beside them.

"God it's hella'va busy in here the 'night," looking around. "Gloria, are you buying?" he asked.

"Aye, two baggies," she replied.

"Angie, two baggies tae?"

"Aye, Joe," said Angie.

"Wee yin?" looking at Cathleen. "Same for you." As he slipped them under the table, he moved around.

"Patsy, I've got your order here, any baggies, hen?"

"Aye, Joe, two the 'night." As he slipped them under the table, at the same time quoting the price, she handed the cash over as they had done. Joe melted away into the crowd.

At the interval, Patsy told Cathleen, "You were really great. Where did you learn to sing like that, hen?"

"At school, Patsy. I had a great music teacher and I was in the choir," she added proudly. "But Mum died when I was twelve and there was nobody to help," she said sadly.

"Changing the subject, girls, when I went to see Aunty today, she was not too good, not well at all."

"That's a shame," said Gloria. "How old is she, Patsy?"

"I think eighty-four, so we don't hold out a lot of hope," she sighed. "Also, I have to be back tomorrow as Mum is not too clever either," lying like a true professional.

"We'll hear how you get on next week. Right girls, time up, work awaits," interrupted Angie.

As they left, Cathleen lamented, "That's a shame you have to go home."

"Never mind, that's life, Cathleen. Remember what I said, get a life, try a few clubs. You could do well, I'm telling you, Cathleen."

"Do you really think so, Patsy?"

"Yes, I do, say nothing to anyone, just do it. Try different towns, even England, come on now, girl. Bye now," Patsy encouraged her.

Next day, on the train, Maddie, dressed as herself, thought, thank goodness it's over. Monday, I will be in my own world. Nice clean, crisp uniform, my colleagues, and Sister to hurry us along. I just hope I don't lose my nerve and let the others down, she told herself.

Chapter 30

Tuesday evening found them all in the flat. Ursula and Glenda were happy Maddie was back safely.

"Firstly, I managed to get the drugs plus a little extra. I had to buy the same amounts they bought. My biggest fear, amongst all the other fears, was any one of them becoming suspicious of me. These people are scary. I must confess, I have become a habitual liar. But my plan for Knox needs a wee bit of advice from you two," said Maddie.

"That's not a bother, Maddie, tell us and then we will all go over it. Take your time," said Ursula.

Maddie continued. "Plan one was to give him an insulin overdose. On the other hand, that would only make him feel better. So I will go for plan two. If I take my own syringe filled with water, that will most likely work. It's how to get it to him that's the problem." She heaved a sigh.

Ursula interrupted. "Maddie, remember he goes for an Indian or a Chinese. They then have a couple of bottles of wine with a heavy meal then go on to the club."

Glenda said, "At the club, I counted. He had seven pints of beer and five whiskies on the Saturday night. And he smokes like a chimney. Is that any help?"

"Well, it is in a way. Diabetics take their short-acting shot mid-morning then the long-acting one at night. The evening one is the one I must change. A guy like him, out wining and dining, might forget to take his mid-morning one. Without his injection he might feel hungry and tired. He might eat a chocolate bar which will push his sugar levels up even further. God alone knows what that amount of booze and fags will do. . . I've not worked that out yet."

Ursula said, "Sounds good so far, Maddie."

"Glenda is the pre-booked taxi driver waiting for me outside the club. I will offer him a lift. That's my only chance to do a swap. When we get to his place, I'll ask can I use his loo. I will exchange his syringe for mine. This is the only loose end I can see but I can't see him refusing a fellow drunk the toilet. I won't go into details but he will not feel too good then go into a coma which he will not awaken from," said Maddie.

"Remember, ladies, his wife goes to her sister's at the weekends so he will be on his own. She will not find him till the Sunday. The beauty of this plan is it does not look like murder. With his lifestyle, he has more or less caused it himself." She paused. "What do you think, ladies?"

"I think it's as good as you can get it," said Ursula. "So what is your problem?"

"I'm worrying if we should do a dummy run tomorrow night," Maddie replied.

"I don't think so, Maddie," said Ursula.

"Nor I," said Glenda. "We stand more chance of being seen twice."

"So, it's on then," Maddie conceded. "I'm not sure what happens next. . . the wife will call an ambulance or doctor. Police will have to be called as it's a sudden death. The doctor will sign the death certificate. If it's his own doctor, he knows he has a drinking problem. I think we should watch carefully to see how it is handled," Maddie explained.

"Sounds like a plan, Maddie. Glenda, you make sure they cannot trace the taxi or driver. Do we have extra number plates for Simon's car?" Ursula asked.

"Yes, we do have two extra, and taxi signs which we only change away from the flat," replied Glenda.

"Good. You two are working well together. If you need anything else, just ask. I will leave on Friday and be away four days which I will probably spend chewing my nails down to the quick.

"Good luck. Remember, ladies, to allow for nerves. Take no risks that can be avoided. This is the real thing, not plans. Look after each other."

They all left the flat in the usual way.

Maddie and Glenda both realised the seriousness of their mission. Though scared half out of their minds. Maddie thought, if I'm truthful with myself, I'm anticipating it with a kind of horrid fascination.

Chapter 31

Glenda's sister, Moira, had organised a wee trip for their mum and Kim. They were booked into a small bed and breakfast in Dunoon. As it was the May weekend, a school holiday, there was lots going on for children. A new, purpose-built hall had laid on lots of indoor and outdoor pursuits.

Glenda drove them to the bus station in Glasgow where they caught the bus to Gourock. From there, they would cross over to Dunoon on the ferry. Kim jumped up and down with excitement.

"Are we going on a boat, Granny?" she asked.

"Yes, sweetie, the bus drives onto the ferry then we sail over to Dunoon."

"Mum, we are going on a big boat." She could hardly contain her excitement. Glenda waved them off as they happily left the station. Her eyes filled with tears as she saw her mother and wee girl happy for a change. We have all lost so much, she pondered.

A taxi was booked at the other end so there were no worries on that score. They stood on the deck as the breeze gently lifted their hair.

"Oh, Granny, this is such an adventure," Kim gasped. "Did you see the seals playing in the water? Have we got a camera with us so we can show them to Mum?" she went on.

"Yes, we have, sweetheart. We are lucky enough to live in one of the most beautiful countries in the world. A tiny jewel in the middle of the Atlantic Ocean. I promise you we will go on many more trips, and the camera is in the suitcase. What do you think, Kim?"

"Great," replied Kim as she giggled.

"Maybe Millport, Rothsay or Oban. We could go bagging islands, just as some people go bagging munros. That's mountains, you know. They can keep their Spain and Portugal, we will see our own first. And, what's more, my lovely, the bus is free for pensioners," as she smiled into Kim's face.

"Yes, yes, Granny," retorted Kim, jumping up and down.

Mrs Marley was delighted to see the wee one happy. It had all been so hard on her baby girl. Also, it might be good for Glenda to spend some time with her friends. She never seemed to stop working.

The Craigieburn Bed and Breakfast was on the front. Their room had the most spectacular view. They settled into their cosy wee room, then a walk along the front looking for somewhere nice for dinner.

Chapter 32

Glenda and Maddie met in the flat about six on Saturday. It seemed so quiet without Ursula who had left yesterday. They were both as nervous as kittens. Ursula had advised them to have something to eat before leaving for their assignment. Maybe a little soup, she had suggested, just to settle their tums.

"Did your mum and Kim get away okay?" Maddie asked, more for something to say as her tongue was stuck to the roof of her mouth. A wee drink might help, she told herself.

"They were fine. Kim was so excited, as if she was going on an adventure."

"Well, you and I are certainly going on an adventure tonight, Glenda," Maddie responded.

"We have waited a while in vain for justice, Maddie. Now we will take it. I'm so glad to have two friends to help and support me," she replied seriously. For a change, Glenda was the confident one.

"Thanks for that, Glenda. Now we have our timetable worked out to the last minute. We will each sit down and have a little hot soup. Then we'll get changed into our working gear. Thank goodness it's not as complicated as Patsy. That took me over an hour to get right. I can still smell that awful perfume," she grinned.

"I'll do mine as well. It's only a slinky top, shiny trousers and a chunky wee jacket. Plus a shoulder length red wig and high heels with a gold trim. Quite classy if I say so myself. It's amazing what changing from brown to red hair can do. I hardly know myself in the mirror," Glenda continued.

Her hands were shaking, Maddie noticed. "Glenda, put a bit extra blusher on your cheeks, you are very pale tonight. You don't want to look peely-wally on a night out, do you?" Maddie advised.

"Maddie, check while I do my checklist."

"Will do," Maddie replied.

"Okay. That's your two water filled syringes. We have cash, phone and gloves. Do we have the short fair wig for when I come back from dropping him off? I have a shoulder-length wig, a plain tee shirt and an anorak for when I become a taxi driver, plus flat shoes.

"That's fine. Everything's complete," Glenda said. "New number plates, taxi signs and two wigs. Also, two jackets in the boot. Do you really think we can pass ourselves off as two ladies just having a wee night out, Maddie?" She took a deep breath.

"Glenda, that is what we are, so tremble no more. We have lift off," she finished grimly.

Chapter 33

Matt Thomson was glad to be home even though it was to that bitch of a wife. Good thing she spent weekends with her equally obnoxious sister, Jean. Another fucking know-it-all. Never mind, they would be off to Australia in four weeks. He forgot to ask for how long, who bloody cares, hope it's for good and the buggers never come back, he contemplated. He had put that wee bit of trouble behind him. He was still a bit sick about that bill. I mean, ten grand that shitbag lawyer, McIntosh, had presented him with. They are the ones getting away with murder. He did next-to-no work. I gave him the lowdown about the machine. I would like to know how much those bastards get an hour to be able to charge that kind of cash. Still, she never seen the bill or that would have been another bloody battle, fucking bitch. Oh, forget the bloody lot of them, he thought.

He had been looking forward to the 'night. The four of them were going out to a slap-up meal. Then back to the club for the rest of the night. It was big Andy's birthday and that meant a right good laugh, he told himself.

Chapter 34

Maddie kept a careful eye on the table the four men were seated at. It was very noisy as they were all talking at once.

"That was a grand dinner at the Indian the 'night," one was telling the other.

"You aye get a really good feed there. I widnae go anywhere else," declared Thomson. "Always good, aye."

Also in the club, waiting, were Maddie and Glenda. Thomson was already a bit worse for wear, thought Glenda.

Looking around and taking stock of the place, Maddie said, "Do you think, Glenda, or should I say Sally, this is a really nice club, beautifully decorated? I expect it would have cost a fortune. It looks as if they have brought professionals in. Just look at the reds and browns with just a dab of gold to highlight it."

"This carpet never came from a bargain basement and those sparkling glasses hanging from the ceiling give the whole place a touch of class, with prices to match, no doubt," commented Glenda.

It appeared to be very busy. Maddie noticed the tables were cleared as soon as drinks were finished. Tips were dependent on that kind of service, she observed. She, however, kept her hands under the table just in case someone noticed them shaking. Luckily for them, people did not pay too much attention to two women out for a drink in peace.

Thomson started his goodnights and cheerios at eleven. That was Glenda's sign to leave.

"Well, goodnight Carol, lovely to see you, after all, it's been a while. Hubby will be waiting outside." She had been practising again in the mirror, waving and smiling as she left.

As Maddie saw Thomson making for the door, she went to the *Ladies* to phone Glenda and advise her to head for club door too.

She bumped into Thomson in the foyer, fumbling to get coins from his pocket to phone a taxi. Her stomach was doing somersaults while her knees had turned to jelly.

"My taxi is here," she said politely. "I could drop you off, save you waiting. Where to?"

"Nelson Court," he replied.

"It's on my way, it's no bother," said Maddie.

"Thanks a lot, hen. I'll half the fare if you like."

"My husband ordered and paid it for me so you're all right," she explained.

"Great, hen," he said.

They went outside and waited for the taxi as Glenda slowly rolled towards them.

Maddie slid over as he struggled to get into the back seat.

"Driver, could you drop this gentleman off at Nelson Court please, and then on to my house? I think you have the address."

"Yes, Madam," responded the driver, "which number?"

"Number sixteen, hen," he answered. "Matt. My name is Matt. I've never seen you at the club before."

"I'm usually with my husband. You most likely will know him if you saw him."

"Aye, hen," he said.

She could see he was tired. No wonder after all he had consumed today. All the better, she thought.

"Do you think I could use your toilet?" she asked.

"No bother, hen," he said. "First on the left."

"Thank you so much," she said pleasantly returning to the front door.

"You're welcome, hen. I need to take my medicine now as I'm dead beat," he said as he closed the door behind her.

She almost flew to the safety of the taxi and sank into the seat beside Glenda, her heart racing. She felt sick. It was over, thank God.

"Are you all right, Maddie?" Glenda asked anxiously, her hands trembling, they would not stay still. "Will you give me a minute to drive, just a wee bit shaky."

"I'm fine. Don't worry, take your time, just a little stressed," answered Maddie. "Oh, hell, that was scary. His medication was in a box in the bathroom, all lined up like toy soldiers. All I had to do was take the insulin on top, put it in my pocket and replace it with the water-filled one I had brought. He would use the first one to hand That was that. I was scared skinny. So, you remember when you do the next one, be aware of how afraid you will be. That's when we can make mistakes, Glenda. Your brain seems to freeze or go on a go-slow. That's the only way I can describe it. The planning is the most important part. To have everything in place, even in our minds, before we start. Lesson learned."

"Oh, Maddie, I would hate to let you down."

"You won't let anyone down. Don't even think like that, Glenda," Maddie reassured her. "We will both go back to the flat for an hour, have a cup of tea and unwind. It's been a hellish day for us both."

Back in the flat with her tea and chocolate biscuit, Glenda confessed, "Maddie, I can't be alone tonight. Put on our tees, put up the recliners and tuck ourselves in for the night. What do you think?"

"Good thinking," was the quick reply.

As they settled, Glenda whispered, "Sometimes, I have this dream about repaying that wee bastard, Shepherd. She more or less got off scot-free. No jail or a fine. Nothing.

"She's out cold in a bed, lying in a strange room. I'm giving her a blood transfusion. Instead of her giving blood, I'm draining hers into a big plastic tub. Which I then pour down the toilet pan. As she gets weaker, I tell her just what she has taken from me. The real cost of losing my child. Maddie, I will never be able to replace my boy. She hurt my Kim. She will have no brother to go through life with. He would have been a comfort to her when Mum and I are gone." She paused, harsh sobs robbing her of breath. "Do you think I'm going mad, Maddie?"

"No way are you going mad, Glenda. Don't ever think that." Maddie went on. "I don't have dreams. I have nightmares which are too evil to repeat. There is no remorse left in me. My girl, Sophie, was my gift to the world. After all, you and I are the result of thousands of years, our ancestors go back to the beginning of time. My genes could have gone on till the end of time through my girl, her children and grandchildren. That bastard robbed me of that. Now he will have to pay. You, me and Ursula will attend to that." Her all-encompassing hatred was frightening to see. "We will feel better, I promise you. These dreams will slowly fade," Maddie almost vowed. "As for now, we will forget for a while, settle down to sleep. Dream of Ursula having a good time in New York, jumping on and off the uptown and downtown buses."

"What bus is that, Maddie?"

"I'll tell you about it another day. Just close your eyes now. Good night, Glenda," Maddie said, turning out the light as they both relived this hellish night, wrapped in their own personal misery.

Chapter 35

Susan Thomson arrived home at about ten-thirty on Sunday. It was a little unusual for Matt not to be up and about. Nonetheless, she didn't give it much thought as she had an ironing to do. An hour later, she went upstairs. He seemed to be asleep as she put away the ironing.

"Matt, it's after eleven. Time to get up," she said.

Leaning over him, she could see he was not breathing and was cold. She could not move for a moment. Then fell back into the bedside chair, trying to think what to do. Will I phone an ambulance, police or doctor?

Gathering her wits about her, she phoned the emergency operator who was very helpful, telling her to sit tight while she phoned for an ambulance.

"Don't put the phone down, Mrs Thomson. I will stay on the line till they arrive. It might be about five minutes. They will take it from there," she said kindly.

The two men were there in no time. One man sat with her in the living room as the other went upstairs. When he came down, he shook his head towards the one with her.

"I'm very sorry, Mrs Thomson, there is nothing we can do. He appears to have passed away in his sleep," he told her.

Susan Thomson looked blankly from one to the other, yet said nothing. They phoned the health centre while she waited for a doctor.

It was not the usual man and when he reappeared downstairs, he asked her, "When did you last see him?"

"I stayed at my sister's last night as he was going to a night out at his club."

"Did he take his medication as prescribed?"

"Yes. Always," she replied.

And then the dreaded question.

"Had he been drinking?"

She was mixed up. How do you tell a stranger she hardly knew what he was doing when on a bender? "Most likely," she answered. Her head was spinning and her mouth dry. "Can I phone my sister?" she asked through trembling lips.

"Of course. I will phone for you," he replied.

"We will be out in the van if you need us," said one of the ambulance crew.

At that, Jean came through the door, pale and worried.

"Are you all right, Susan?" as she took her hand and hugged her.

"They didn't tell me much, just that Matt had passed away in his sleep." Now Jean was here, Susan burst into tears. They sat together on the couch while the house filled with people. The doctor and a nurse had a look at her.

"Are you feeling sick or dizzy at all, Mrs Thomson, as we can give you something if you are?" he explained.

"No, I'm fine," she sobbed.

As they left, two policemen came in. They introduced themselves.

"I am DS Andrew McNeil and my colleague is Constable Alan Starrs," said one of them. "We have a few questions for you then we will leave and come back tomorrow when you are more settled," he said. He asked almost the same as the doctor.

"I don't know very much that would help you," she replied softly. She felt sick, and very hot. The house seemed to be full of strange men. A lady was in her kitchen making tea. Who is she? She thought. Then she realised it was Shona, her next door neighbour. God Almighty, she mused, it's like a merry-go-round in here.

Jean arrived with some overly sweet tea, at the same time handing her two paracetamols. "Take these, dear. They will help to calm you," she went on, putting the tea down.

She was vaguely aware of the ambulance men going upstairs. Shona sat beside her while Jean went upstairs, closing the door behind her so she could not see what was happening.

Suddenly, it was very quiet.

Chapter 36

Ursula was on the early flight from New York to London, three hours stopover, then on to Glasgow. It had been a nice break, nonetheless, her thoughts had never been too far from her ladies. At the hotel, she had met two women. Acting normal had been difficult.

"I'm Ursula," she told them.

"I'm Sarah and this is my friend, Elizabeth, and this is our first trip to the USA," replied the older one.

"We want to see it all," Elizabeth told her.

Well that's lucky, thought Ursula. If I tag along, show them the ropes, so to say, that might keep me busy and keep my mind off the business at home.

"Your best plan is to get the uptown bus and then the downtown bus the next day. You can then jump on and off where you want to. You will see Chinatown, Central Park, also the garment district. You might also like Times Square which has quite a few small theatres as well as the big ones."

"Oh great," they chorused. "We'll go to Saks from there and get our faces made up for free before going out to dinner."

They stopped to have their shoes shined and took photos. The bus took them to Harlem. The bus driver warned, "Better not to get off here, Ma'm."

"I did not realise there were so many churches here and choirs singing outside," exclaimed Sarah.

"Well, it is Baptist country, this end of town," laughed Ursula. "I think you would be better buying postcards than taking photos."

"I didn't know New York was so big," said Sarah.

"A good idea is to buy a jigsaw puzzle of America, where all the states are different colours. That gives you an idea of size. You could fit Scotland into some states," smiled Ursula. Heavens, she thought, as she waved them cheerio on the last day, they are just like teenagers.

On the flight home, her imagination worked overtime, terrified for her girls. God, give yourself peace, before you have a stroke, she scolded herself.

Ruth came to the airport to collect her. Ursula was happy to be home, surrounded by familiar things. She touched the framed photograph of Simon, running her fingers lovingly over his face.

"I'll go and get a little shopping for you, Mum. You have a wee rest after that long flight. Did you have a nice time? More important, I hope you enjoyed yourself. We were worried about you going alone."

"No need to. I met two extremely nice women, besides which, we were chummed together for the weekend," Ursula added, as if it had all been great fun.

No sooner was Ruth out the door than she was on the phone to Maddie.

"How did it all go?" she gasped.

Maddie was so glad to hear her voice, she almost cried.

"Tell you what, I'll meet you after work at your niece, Cathleen's flat. Will you phone Glenda for me? You don't have to worry, we finished making up her new curtains and we hung them up for her," she answered.

Ursula could hardly breathe. "That's so kind of you both. She will be so pleased, thank you so much. I will settle up with you later."

Next, Glenda's number.

"Hello dear, Maddie tells me you finished Cathleen's curtains and put them up for her, so very nice of you both. I'm meeting her at six if that's any use to you?"

Glenda could hardly stop herself from babbling. Breathe slowly, take your time, she told herself.

"That would be no bother at all," she replied as calmly as she could manage. "Thank you," she added. At the same time, her heart was playing a little tune against her ribs.

Chapter 37

"Mum, would you mind staying a wee bit longer tonight as someone has called in sick?" Glenda asked her mother.

"Not a bother, I will stay tonight. Kim calls it a sleepover," Mrs Marly replied, happy not to go home to her lonely wee house. We are working on the notes for our photo album from Dunoon." Kim and Granny had lots in common after their fun trip.

The ladies met at six.

"I don't know where to start," Ursula sighed heavily. "There is no firm confirmation of Thomson's demise. It's bound to be in the Times tonight or tomorrow. I may hear from one of my colleagues at work. We will just have to wait. Coffee first then tell me all that happened on Saturday."

"We learned a lot, Ursula. We might have to reconsider the nerves element as we were both terrified out of our wits. Planning and taking notes is one thing. I admit, having it rehearsed and organised is a help. The real thing is a different ball game. Waiting was hell. Also my mind seemed to freeze. You have to physically will yourself to continue. My hands would not stop shaking. The thudding of my heart was the overall sensation. When I went back to the car with Glenda, everything shook. I felt sick with fear. Being part of a team helps plus we took comfort in one another.

"The club part was fine. I offered him a lift and he accepted. First hurdle over. In the house, I went to the loo, hurdle two. The loo was very tidy and his medication was in place. It was just a case of swapping the syringes. I almost ran out the door to be honest, Ursula. He was glad to see the back of me. He must have felt extremely tired at that point. Just thinking about it makes my knees knock."

"Thank you, Maddie. We will keep those observations in mind. Thank you. What are your thoughts and feelings, Glenda?" she asked.

"I would agree with all Maddie said, Ursula. Nerves were a problem. Every little bit of me shook, even my voice. Having each other in the same boat was a plus. I would add the dressing up bit helped. You are not yourself. You are playing a role. Dressed as a girl on a night out, that was what I was. Same driving the taxi. I was a taxi driver. Haven't got a clue how it works but it does," she added.

"That's a useful insight into that aspect of it, Glenda, I have to admit, never giving a thought to that. Well done, ladies.

"The long weekend in New York was fine. I chummed up with two women from Perth which took my mind off you two. However, I never stopped worrying. As you both now know, your imagination is far worse than the real thing. We'll talk about it some other time. We are too uptight to enjoy listening to other people having fun," she continued.

Glenda agreed. "It's the same listening to Mum and Kim about their great adventure. Also the ones they are planning. Trying to smile and laugh is the difficult part. It was nice to see them giggling together though. I could never begrudge them that small pleasure," Glenda said. Looking up, she leaned over, squeezing Maddie's hand. Seeing her despondency was awful. She had no one. They glanced at one another.

Ursula, seeing the empathy between them, smiled inwardly. Her girls were bonded. The circle she had created was tight, welded solid, unbreakable.

Glenda, changing the subject, looked at Maddie. "I meant to ask, what was that man like, up close?"

"I can only say he was the most selfish, obnoxious and unpleasant person it's been my misfortune to meet. In addition, in my opinion, the world is well rid of him. They could hold his funeral in a phone box, as my Granny used to say. That's how many friends that bastard has," she retorted bitterly.

Oh dear me, time for a sharp exit from that topic, thought Ursula.

"My main worry, while in America, was the ever-present danger of being caught. That must be our first and last concern. If for any reason, you feel uneasy about any enterprise you're involved in, drop everything and leave immediately. Ladies, I can't stress that enough," she continued.

"There was a lot of talk about the increase in the police presence. Up in Dundee, the dealers are being extra careful. As they put it, the bloody polis are everywhere there's something going on," said Maddie. "Those guys can smell trouble," she added.

"They seem to know best," said Ursula. "I'll meet you here on Friday as we will need to organise for Allison Shepherd. Also tailing her. This one will be a lot more difficult. We can't use drugs, so it's thinking caps on. Also, Glenda, your trip will have to be finalised.

"Night, girls, and thank you." She was so glad to see them. The fact that they were safe was a bonus. Though she had to admit she was exhausted. Now for the planning for Knox. He appeared to be a nasty, selfish little bugger. This week would see what the wee creep got up to.

Well, off to bed, she told herself.

Chapter 38

DS Andrew McNeil looked again at the information before him. As far as he could see, Matt Thomson had been well over the alcohol limit and furthermore had not taken his medication the previous evening. His GP had said Thomson was known to be a heavy drinker. In addition, he had been warned how dangerous it was for him as a diabetic. The doctor who had attended to him stated his medication was in the bathroom but maybe Thomson had forgotten to take it. His wife admitted he often went on benders when he came home.

McNeil handed his report to DI John Diamond. He read through it. Not a lot to it really.

"Did you visit the house, Andrew?" he asked.

"Yes I did. Mrs Thomson told us she was visiting her sister's the previous night. It's a case of the usual old story, when he's on a bender, she stays with her sister," McNeil said.

DI Diamond read the report again.

"I agree, the usual – too much booze and too much money. This guy is a well-known boozer. Word on the street is he has been in bother a couple of times before for driving over the limit. When the hell will they learn?"

"Did you know him, Sir?" asked McNeil.

"No, but I know plenty like him. Just leave it there. I'll have Amy file it. Thanks a lot, Andrew."

DI Diamond sat back, deep in thought. There were too many of these guys who thought they could drink and drive, showing no concern for other people. Not even a second thought for their families. In his opinion, too much police time was wasted on them. A much bigger problem was the amount of drugs floating about. Along with the criminal element who controlled them. He thought they needed to look a bit further with the suppliers. They could always nab the wee guys. Nonetheless, it's the big boys they needed to stop. A much more concerted effort might be needed. It wasn't only the drugs but the rubbish they were out with. One young copper had remarked that you could bake a cake with the amount of baking powder that some baggies contained.

    He laughed to himself.

Chapter 39

At the Friday meeting, Glenda, who had been fretting, stated, "Waiting is the hardest part."

Matt Thomson's body had not been released until two days after his death.

"Do you think he was having a post-mortem?" said Glenda.

Ursula raised both hands to reassure them. "Listen, ladies, stop this unnecessary worrying. Even if there was a PM, what would they find? That his blood was ninety proof. The only thing that would set alarm bells off was if he left an empty syringe at the bedside, it was found and tested. . . then finding no medication in it," Ursula continued.

Maddie explained, "I noticed there was a sharps box near the box of medication. Also, his wife is extremely tidy. I can't see her allowing him to leave these things lying about. Most people are extremely careful with syringes. Additionally, he has been diabetic for a number of years," she said.

"A lot of needless worry," agreed Ursula. "Take into account the element of guilt, which may make us a bit stressed. To be honest, guilt is not the word I would use so much as elated."

A small giggle escaped from Glenda and Maddie.

"This week we have such a lot to do. You will have to make a decision who will be first. Knox or Shepherd.

"I think it should be Knox. The reason being, Glenda and I will tail him and see what he is doing these days. To my mind, Shepherd will be more difficult as she is not a drug addict. So, a completely new plan for her. Glenda, remember, drop a wee hint at home to Mum and Kim about their trip and also yours, with your sister. Is Rome still your choice? I would like to do this one in the next few weeks. Maddie, are you still planning for Paris?"

"Yes. I would like Paris. Besides, Mum has never been. She seems to think I am doing a bit better lately."

"You *are* looking a bit more cheerful, Maddie. Not so silent and miserable. I think it's those new counsellors you are seeing.

"So, take a bow, ladies. I have to admit, it went better than I hoped, with a bit of luck thrown in. But don't depend on luck. It's over and done with. No going over in our minds what might have been.

"Glenda, you do the evenings and see what Knox is about. Your Mum thinks you are at bereavement class on Thursday and Friday. I'll do afternoons and Saturday. Meet here on Sunday. Maddie, if you have time, do a bit of snooping the Shepherd woman. See what she is all about. You could maybe drop a wee hint to Mum about planning a wee trip. See what she fancies," she went on. "That's it for today. It's been a learning curve for us all, that's for sure. By the way, Glenda, do we need any more wigs or are we okay?" Ursula said.

"We are fine for everything, Ursula, so far at least," Glenda replied. "When I go to the baths, at first, I will be an onlooker, as if I'm taking my own child. Then, I'll see how the land lies. While next time, I'll be a cleaner. What do you think?"

"Fine," answered Ursula. "You'll be wanting to go into films next, Glenda," trying to lift the nervous mood which had threatened to overwhelm them. "So, off we go and try and get a good night's sleep," thinking Glenda had been worrying. I know just how she feels.

Setting the ladies' minds at ease, Matt Thomson's funeral took place the week after he was brought home. His son and daughter-in-law had flown home from Australia to attend and comfort his mother. Many who attended did not know about his 'wee problem' so the event was quite respectable. Ursula had heard about it at school. Nothing much was said, just the bare facts. She never even answered the lady who told her, who knew better to say no more.

Chapter 40

James Knox believed he was the one hard done by. It was a mistake okay, he told himself. He had served his time. To his mind, that should have been the end of it. But no, he still had nine months on license as well, fuck. At his prison medical, they'd discovered a slight heart condition. Not serious but it would need to be watched. Some mess, he lamented. Still, his wee pal, Mick, got his baggies for him. If caught buying, he was back in the nick, shit. Good job the old man disnae know about the two in his sock draw. That guy never stops nagging and he watches my every move. Man, I'm fucking pissed off wi that bugger, so I am. The old lady's just as bad, treating me like a wean, she can bugger off tae.

Before that wee mistake, I was having the time of my life. Flash car, plenty of lassies, clubbing and pubbing every weekend. Great holidays with the lads in Spain and no ties, free as a bird. Living at home, cheap as chips, working with Dad as a joiner with the council, good money tae.

Then, wham-bam, all gone in minutes. Doing forty-eight in a thirty limit was not a smart move after a drink and a baggie. I didnae mean to hit the wee lassie or the old wumman. I didnae see them. Not sure how much I'd had to drink but the polis said twice over the limit. But you know them polis, bloody liars tae a man.

The wee baggie didnae help. The bloody fuss the paper made added to the mess. Calling me a drunken thug, whit a bloody cheek, it was a first offence. My God, that court case was pure murder. Everybody looking at me as if I was a piece of shit. Them lawyers discussing me like I wisnae there.

Right enough, I felt a wee bit sorry for the wee lassie's family. My mother looking at them with a strange look. Worse of all, the young mother, pale as death, looking straight at me, her eyes pools of contempt and naked hatred. I'll never forget that look. Oh man.

Nae car, or good job, now in the council garden department. Hell, you needed wheels to work in the joinery shop.

Shit, whit I need is a wee night out. I'll only have three pints or greeting face will start moaning the second I'm in the door. Oh hell, whit a bloody life.

Chapter 41

Tuesday evening, Glenda parked near the council garden department. She hated waiting but needs must. Three young guys appeared, Knox among them. He was carrying a rolled-up towel. She surmised they were headed for the local swimming baths. She followed, parking further up the road. As they went in, she stood outside pretending to smoke a cigarette. What a stink, she mused, my tracksuit and lovely auburn wig would reek. Going inside, buying two tickets, one adult, one child. She then made her way to the seating, making sure she was alone, not a time for making friends. Keeping her hands in her pockets as they shook quite badly. She did not know why she was so nervous as this was only tailing, nonetheless, she was. Maybe because she was on her own.

Watching them for maybe ten minutes while they appeared to be enjoying themselves. She made her way to the ladies. To the left there was a room with lockers full of cleaning materials. Also, a few overalls hanging on hooks. She noticed there were cubicles, male on one side and females on the other. There were also two shower rooms at the exit to the pool. Knox and pals' clothes were hanging up in the three end cubicles. As she passed the cleaners' cupboards, she put her head around the door. Tubs of chemicals, boxes of rubber gloves were stacked up neatly. But more important, no one stopped her, inquiring what she was doing, even better. That did not stop her heart racing and knees knocking. She made her way quickly back to the benches to fill her notebook. She knew how important it was to keep a careful note of the time. Ten minutes to change and shower before the swim and the same after the swim. They were in the pool thirty minutes. As far as she could see, that gave the ladies a clear thirty minutes to plant whatever Maddie had for them. As they were leaving the pool, she made her way back to the car where she did some breathing exercises to calm herself. As the boys stopped at the pub, she made her way home to Mum and Kim and normality.

Ursula did her tailing on Thursday. Glenda had phoned with an outline of her tour of the baths. She parked along the road at the garden department then followed the lads to the pool. She was already dressed as a cleaning lady. A grey wig and black trousers with blue overall, she had brought her own rubber gloves. Better not to take any chances. The guys followed the same routine as Tuesday. They went to the cubicles and shower room then the pool. Going into the cleaners' room was a bit more nerve-racking as she was not too sure who or what she would find. It was silent and empty. There were large gallon bottles of cleaning fluid and lots of boxes of stuff. She had brought her cleaning cloths with her so proceeded to the cubicles and cleaned them. Also, the ladies' toilets and showers. She smiled to herself as she wondered what the real cleaners would think when they seen a fairy had done their work in the night. She would have to remind Glenda to take careful note of what each guy was wearing. No mix-ups. Again, they were in the pool the same time so she made for her car. Once more, they went to the pub so she made her way home. Before bed, she wrote up her notebook.

On Sunday, they met in the flat at one. As they relaxed over coffee, both Ursula and Glenda had their notebooks ready.

"I had to put my tracksuit into the cleaners; the smell was awful. I think I'll change to menthol cigs in future."

"Good idea, Glenda," said Maddie.

"I see what you ladies mean about nerves. My mouth was so dry I could hardly swallow. Next time, I'll have a wee sweetie to suck," said Ursula. "Now, down to business. This Tuesday and Thursday, we tail him. We have to note what he is wearing and if there is a baggie in his inside pocket. Also, listen and try and find out if he is going clubbing on Friday.

The following Friday is when he will most likely use the doctored baggie. We cannot be sure if he takes it on Friday or Saturday in the club," she went on. "It doesn't matter to us as long as we are well clear, okay?"

"Fine," said Maddie. "I have read up on it and the police are more than worried about the number of teenage deaths due to drugs. Word is, there is a bad batch in circulation. Knox uses cocaine so I will add a wee bit something to his baggie. Most likely heroin. I have both, so no worries there."

"I'll leave that to you, Maddie. Now the other thing is, you will have to leave on the Thursday and back on the Monday. Are you still happy with Rome? Are you taking your sister?"

"Yes. I'll break the news as if it's a wee surprise to cheer us both up," she replied.

"That's enough for today. We have quite a bit to think about. Maddie, maybe you should have a wee sniff about that Shepherd woman this week."

"No bother," Maddie agreed, giving Glenda a swift sympathetic glance.

"Right ladies, home for a family lunch today. I'm going to Ruth's for a bite. Showing her how well I am doing."

Chapter 42

Monday, Maddie finished work early. I'll go and investigate where Allison Shepherd is. She'd heard the young doctor had been moved to another department. Most likely, where she can do less harm. It gets me down, thought Maddie, the way things are not so much covered up as glossed over. In her ward, Sister would have your head in your hands for so much less. There wasn't much more she could find out here. A young nurse gave her Shepherd's address in Lenzie.

"My cousin is one of her flatmates so it's okay to give it to you," she explained.

Maddie drove over to Lenzie, not quite knowing what she would say if Shepherd was in. Hopefully she would be at work. Knocking the door, her nerves all a tingle, while she waited. It was opened by a young lady.

"My name is Sarah Harvey, a friend of Allison. Is she in?" she lied. "I'm down from Dundee for a few days. I thought I might catch up."

"I'm her flatmate, Anne, you've not long missed her. Allison and our other flatmate, Greta, are away looking for a new car for Allison, well, nearly new," she informed Maddie.

"Sorry to have missed her. I'll try and call back tomorrow evening on my way home. You could maybe let her know I called," Maddie continued.

"Yes, no bother," said the girl pleasantly.

"Bye then and thank you," Maddie replied. Ursula would be pleased with that little nugget of information. A new car, my, she thought. I wonder how Ursula is doing as the cleaning lady at the pool.

At that moment, Ursula was busy changing into her grey wig, overall and black trousers for her new job at the pool. As this was her third day here, she was feeling fairly confident. Making her way into the cleaners' room, her heart almost stopped with fright as another lady was already there.

"Hallo," the woman said. "Are you new here?"

"Yes," replied Ursula. "Just for two weeks then I go to Kirkintilloch Baths," she fibbed.

"I'm Sally," the woman answered, "and I'm running a wee bit late tonight."

"My name is Liz," said Ursula, her heart beating a drum beat against her ribs. She took the clean wash cloths from the cupboard and moved around to the male cubicles where she started dusting the seats, hooks and doors down. Keep calm, she told herself, it's okay, no need to panic. At the same time, she could feel the cold sweat trickle down her back. Ten minutes later, Sally called out to her.

"I'm off, Liz, see you again," and was gone.

Ursula's legs could hardly move. She had to sit for a second or two, trying to gather her wits.

Check the boys are in the pool. Then check Knox's jacket. It was a casual one tonight but it still had an inside pocket which was empty. Good.

Waiting another five minutes, she removed her overall and left, using the front door. She had to sit in the car a wee while to calm herself enough to drive. Pulling her wig off as she drove away, she was herself again.

Chapter 43

Sunday at the flat was the last catching up day before the big day on Thursday, the same day Maddie would go on her break so there was a lot to go through.

"Do we have all we need, Glenda?" Ursula asked.

"Yes," replied Glenda. We already have our new wigs and overalls and when we leave the baths, it's straight home. We have no need to follow them to the club. New plates are in the car. I'll change them before I leave."

"I have the special baggie here. Remember there is only one, so be careful. Knox is a stupid guy who takes crack before going for a drink, after the baths. He has a lot more at the club for his 'big high'. I have put a mixer in his cocaine. It doesn't matter if he takes it Friday or Saturday as long as he takes it and we are well clear," Maddie explained.

"Also, Maddie, are you organised for your trip?"

"Yes," said Maddie. "My sister, Moira, is going with me as she can get time off work and is happy to go to help cheer me up. I will be back Monday. The hotel has an assortment of trips and sights to see. I can hardly believe I am going to Rome."

"I would buy a wee book on Rome. You can then work out where you might like best. Also, try and eat in small family-owned restaurants where the food is usually delicious," advised Ursula.

"Now to planning for Thursday. Glenda and I will do the deed. Maddie, you write times and dates for him. Also, start a new board for Shepherd," said Ursula.

"I started tailing Shepherd yesterday. In fact, I've written my findings on my notepad. Next week will do to catch up on her," added Maddie.

"Glenda, are we happy with our plans? The fact it will still be daylight when we go to the pool and lots of people around might be a problem. However, we will just have to deal with anything that turns up. I have to admit, I almost died of fright when that woman was in the cleaners' room, but never mind."

Maddie handed over the baggie to Ursula. Even handling it gave her the creeps.

"That's about all we can do for now. Glenda, you go on Tuesday. The final rehearsal, so to speak. You are the taxi driver and I will put the baggie in his inside pocket," said Ursula. Her mind was in a spin trying to remember everything. "Maddie, you go on your break and try and enjoy yourself. Phone me on Monday to catch up."

"Best of luck to you both. Hopefully all will go well. Stay safe, ladies. Remember your advice to us, Ursula," added Maddie.

At that, it was goodbyes, they left as usual, one by one.

Chapter 44

On Thursday, Glenda and Ursula met at the flat. Both were extremely nervous.

"The waiting is always the hard part," said Glenda.

"I'll go over everything so we know what order we keep to," Ursula explained. "Hopefully the rest of the cleaning ladies will be finished when I arrive. You will remain in the car. Wear your long auburn wig and warm jacket as taxi drivers have a lot of waiting around." She paused, thinking things over.

"Maddie gave me the baggie. She says he might not be used to the fifty percent as they buy twenty-five percent on the street. She says he thinks he's invincible. They take this stuff followed by drink and then a wee top-up. She has added something. So he will be playing with fire with this mixture plus booze. She can't see him surviving this lot. Also, we can't be sure when he will take it, Thursday or Friday."

They both thought about that, the long wait they both dreaded. It had been a nerve-racking wait, wondering if they were going to give it a miss this week.

"But no, it's all go," Glenda gasped as she saw them rolling into the car park.

"Thank goodness," said Ursula, breathing a sigh of relief.

Glenda moved the car forward, dropping Ursula, now addressed as Liz, at the door. Moving off to park in the next street for ten minutes.

Ursula went into the baths, straight for the broom cupboard, taking out a mop, some fresh dusters and cleaning cloths. Going into the ladies', giving all the sinks a wash with the wipes, careful to take her time. Lucky for her, most of the cubicles were full tonight. Knox and his mates had the end three. She had been careful to note his jacket was a black blazer type while the other two had casual jackets. Maddie had checked last week which pocket he kept his stuff in. It was the inside pocket with a zip. Pretending to mop, it was the work of seconds to remove his bag and replace it with hers.

It took all the nerve she possessed to walk slowly back along the row. Replacing the mop and dusters back in the broom cupboard. Going to the ladies, removing her wig and overall, putting them into her fold-up bag. She went out to the front to sit and watch the swimmers calling out to each other.

No one had noticed anything out of the ordinary. Making her way out to the front and quickly out of the front door. Her legs were like jelly. She now knew how the ladies had felt after Matt Thomson. She was never so glad to see anybody as she was to watch Glenda slowly rolling towards her.

Getting in, she said, "Give me a minute, Glenda. I'm shaking all over."

"Don't worry. Take your time. That's the way we were. So it's back to the flat as it takes a wee while to wear off, Ursula."

"That was the most scary time of my life. The waiting is absolute hell," responded Ursula.

Back at the flat, each holding a strong coffee, they went over the day's events. As far as possible, things had gone to plan. This time, it would be a nightmare waiting for the result.

"He could take ill at the club or just waiting for a taxi. On the other hand, he might make it home and sleep away. We have no way of knowing, Ursula."

Ursula pointed out, "We will have to wait and see. Nothing else can be done now. Another thing, we cannot be sure if he takes it on Thursday, Friday or even Saturday," she went on.

"It is over now," said Glenda.

"I will cook some dinner for us," Ursula said kindly.

"Not for me thanks. Maybe a tin of soup. I will have to go home as my mum will worry that I'm working too long. Maddie and I stayed the night here last time but I told Mum I would be home. Will you stay here or go home, Ursula?" Glenda asked.

"I will go home. I like to be with familiar things when I'm troubled," she answered. She was, as Glenda put it, scared skinny tonight. Home was a comfort, she told herself.

Chapter 45

James Knox had left the club quite late. He ordered a taxi for himself, telling his mates he felt awful. They advised him to go straight home. No way did he want to bump into his old man as he would only start his nagging, so he slipped upstairs and into bed without any fuss from them.

On Saturday morning, Mrs Knox called him a few times then asked his father to go up and waken him.

"That laddie gets worse, lying in his bed half the day," he complained as he climbed the staircase.

Opening the blinds there was still no movement, so he pulled back the duvet. Neil Knox knew immediately his son was not asleep; he was very white and cold as ice.

"Oh my God almighty!" he gasped as he slumped down on the bedside chair. "How the hell will I tell his mother, her pride and joy, her only child?" His head dropped into his hands in despair. He went downstairs, pale as a ghost, towards his wife.

"What's wrong, Neil?" she asked, puzzled at her normally calm husband.

"It's James, it's James. I think he has died in his sleep."

"What do you mean? How can that be, he is only young?" she said irrationally as the colour left her face. She put her hands out to him, looking up at him, almost trying to read his face.

"I will phone for an ambulance and I don't want you to go upstairs."

He made the call, returning to his wife. "The ambulance will be here in a wee while to help us. They will tell us what to do," he said as they sat huddled together, waiting.

The paramedics were so nice and took over. One went upstairs while the other questioned them and phoned for a doctor, who said they would be there as soon as possible.

"You do know the police will have to be informed, as in all cases of a sudden death," he explained.

The couple did not know but nodded just the same.

"Neil, did you tell them it's not a serious heart condition James had?"

"I think that will be up to the doctor to decide on these things. It takes a while to find out why he died."

"We will stay with you till the doctor comes. Then we will wait outside while the police investigate as his body cannot be moved till they see it," he explained gently.

At that, his mother's loud sobs filled the room. Neil Knox placed his arm around her. He felt helpless and very much alone.

Chapter 46

When DI Diamond and DS McNeil arrived at the Knox house it was bustling. A doctor, who introduced himself as Dr Ford, was there and a nurse. Two ladies were in the kitchen and appeared to be making tea. Also two ambulance men waited outside.

One lady told him, "Mr and Mrs Knox are in the living room," as she helpfully opened the door for them.

DS McNeil thanked her as they entered.

"Are you the parents of the young man?"

They both just nodded.

"I am DI John Diamond and this is my colleague, DS Andrew McNeil. We will not keep you too long, just a few questions. Firstly, we offer our condolences."

"Mr Knox, did you find your son?"

"Yes," he answered. He was very pale and had his arm around his wife. She appeared to be lost.

"What time was that?" Diamond asked.

"It was after tea, I think. He was out at the club last night and most likely came in late. I never heard him come in," he added.

"I thought I heard him," his mother said. "I can never settle till I know he's home. It was about eleven-thirty or so," she explained.

"That's fine," said Diamond. "I'll have a word with the doctor upstairs."

"He had a prior heart condition but the doctor said it was not serious, just that they would keep an eye on him," his father went on. "Do you think it was maybe worse than they thought?" he asked, puzzled.

"When the doctors at the morgue have finished and I have a report, we will come back and explain it to you," DI Diamond said kindly. He had a few words with Dr Ford who then left. He told the ambulance men they could remove the young man. They went into the living room while the men were bringing him down, telling the parents, "Once again, we are extremely sorry for your loss."

It was one of the jobs they both did not care for. Always glad when it was over.

Chapter 47

Maddie and her sister, Moira, arrived in Rome in time for a late lunch. Maddie had spent the flight with her stomach knotted with worry over her two friends who would be very busy. They were booked into the Hotel Diana, from where you could walk down to the Trevi Fountain.

"It was built for the Emperor Augustus by his son-in-law, Agrippa, to supply water for the Roman Baths in 19BC," explained Maddie to Moira. "Imagine, all that time. It is so beautiful," said Maddie. "Remember to throw your coin in, Moira. It's to ensure you return to Rome."

"Rome has not seen the last of me," her sister assured her. Never would they forget sitting outside sipping a real coffee from tiny cups. Small shops lined the streets selling everything from fridge magnets to expensive handbags.

"Think I'll buy Mum one of these silk scarves with *'Roma'* printed on it," said Maddie.

"Maybe she would like these elegant leather gloves to match," mused Moira.

"She will love them," said Maddie. "I like the way whole families go to lunch together. We should do that more often," as a small wave of sadness passed through her, remembering Sophie and her out to lunch.

A concert in a local church that evening cheered her a little. While Sunday saw them climb the Spanish Steps. Then, joining the Romans in their ritual of promenade, dressed in their best.

"It has been a fabulous trip, Maddie. Thank you so much for taking me. I would never have been able to go on my own. Thank you again."

On the plane home, Maddie's thoughts returned to Ursula and Glenda. How had they managed? Had anything gone wrong? Her legs were doing a dance of their own while her head thumped and cold sweat trickled down her back. Stop it, she told herself, soon be back and catch up. Please God let them both be safe, she prayed silently.

Chapter 48

DI Diamond and DS McNeil returned to Mr and Mrs Knox.

"Come in and have a seat," Mr Knox gestured politely for them to sit.

"We have been worried sick," he explained, "quite honestly, we can't understand how it could have happened. He was a lad who wanted for nothing, being our only child. He was well looked after all his life."

His wife nodded in agreement.

DI Diamond said, "To let you understand, Mr Knox, we are dealing with a very serious drug problem just now. Not only in Glasgow but in all the large cities. Your son, James, had taken a drug overdose along with a considerable amount of alcohol. Mr Knox, your son is the third young man to die in this way in the last three weeks. We think maybe there is a bad batch being sold. The same stuff was in Edinburgh about four months ago when we lost four young people to the exact same mixture."

"Both parents looked at him uncomprehendingly as they turned a ghastly shade of pale but remained silent.

The policeman continued.

"Seemingly, the drug dealers, who make vast profits, hold tight control over the men who work for them. In other words, no one is talking to us." DI Diamond then said, "We can only wait to get firm confirmation from our lab and forensic department. Then we can go public on this matter. At the moment we appear to be fighting a losing battle.

"DS McNeil and I can only offer you our sincere condolences. However, we will get back to you when we can."

Back in the office, the two policemen went over what they had. DS McNeil had now interviewed three of the young men's parents. Two liked to drink and club it but the third, Ian Reid, was a well-known addict who had never held a job, whereas the other two had decent jobs and lived with their parents.

DS McNeil told Diamond, "James Knox had been in prison for a drink-driving charge. He had also had a small amount of drugs in his system then. He had caused a fatality. A little girl. However, he had never previously been in any kind of trouble. Did his time and was out on licence. To my mind, his change of lifestyle, loss of a good job, a flat and his car could be blamed for his drug addiction. As you are well aware, Sir, prison can cause this. This is where they learn, we've seen it all before."

Diamond looked over the report. "You know, Andrew, it gets you down after a while, watching these young men throwing their lives away over drink and drugs. I wish I could get through to them, yet it seems impossible. I just hope there will be no more of these senseless deaths in Glasgow. They give no thought to their parents who are left devastated and most times, unable to understand," he added. "The chief constable has put a warning in the newspapers that may help."

"Yes, Sir," went on DS McNeil. "Maybe we could do a few school talks. I feel that helps but it is the usual, not enough men or money. Even if it saves one life it could be worth it," he finished.

Chapter 49

Sunday saw the three ladies in the flat.

"Coffee first, I have a light lunch for later. On the other hand, we have quite a bit of catching up to do. Did you enjoy Rome, Maddie?" Ursula inquired.

"My sister said it was magical but I was really not in the right frame of mind to appreciate it. But first I would like to hear how you two managed. I didn't sleep the first night for worrying about you ladies. Furthermore, in my dreams, and on the plane, everything that could have gone wrong did go wrong. You were right, Ursula, imagination is worse than reality," Maddie revealed.

"If she thought Rome was magical, just wait till she gets to Paris or Venice," answered Ursula, trying to cheer her a little.

"Now, back to basics," continued Ursula. "Nearly everything went according to plan, however, there was a lot more waiting time between moves. I nearly died of fright when one cleaner was late leaving and I walked into her. She was so engrossed with her own problems, she didn't bother too much with me, thank goodness. It makes you think though. Your nerves are on edge all the time.

"The waiting gets you down, waiting for them to arrive, not sure if they will come; waiting to see how long they'll be in the pool. The worst thing is not knowing if it has worked," she sighed. "I heard a whisper in the local shop about a drug overdose. But we need something from the newspapers or the police. It's a case of waiting once again. Now, for some lunch," said Ursula.

"I think the Shepherd woman is going to be a lot more difficult. She is not a diabetic or a drug addict. Do you have any ideas, Ursula, what we can do with her?" said Maddie.

"We will need to think extremely carefully about that one. The last thing we need is for the police to become suspicious and start investigating much more thoroughly. Also, the drug situation in Britain has become a big problem. The crooks who run drugs are very powerful, along with this they have vast amounts of cash to spend," declared Ursula. "Well, the Knox business is over now. I think in retrospect, we would be wise to wait a while before we tackle Shepherd. What do you ladies think?" Ursula contended.

"But not any longer than four weeks," Glenda agreed. "The strain on us might be more than we can cope with."

"You know, Glenda, you have hidden talents," Maddie added. "I would have rushed in within two weeks, but you are correct, wait and see. Good thinking."

They were almost finished when, quite unexpectedly, Ursula declared, "You know how you girls worry about bad dreams and action replays. I can't say I thought too much about that before. Now, I must confess, I have been having the same as you two.

"It's about that lawyer, you remember the one who got Matt Thomson off. He was a devious swine. My dreams are full of him, some dire punishment for him. I can't get it out of my mind. Maybe, ladies, when we have dealt with Shepherd, we could dream up a wee accident for him. It would really ease my mind," she went on.

They both looked at her, absolutely dumbstruck, as if she had dropped a bombshell.

"Do you really mean that?" said Glenda.

"Yes, I do. He is every bit as guilty as the stupid men he defends, only he does it for profit," she said very calmly.

Maddie thought, "Oh, shit!"

"You mean as a wee extra treat for us," Maddie conceded. "Ursula, you are very naughty," she teased.

Chapter 50

DI Diamond and DS McNeil sat in Diamond's office. The report on James Knox appeared to match the other two young men, Ian Reid and Thomas Kelly, who had both died from drug overdoses. All had died from cocaine mixed with heroin, nearly always a deadly combination, to those in the know: *Screwballs*.

"It's unusual, Sir," said McNeil, most of these guys use sugar or powdered milk or baking soda as mixers. They are cheaper. After all, money is the name of the game. I suspect someone has just made a mistake or is just starting out."

"Just in case, Andrew, I would have a wee nosey around the club. See if you see any well-known faces. It might be worthwhile. Robertson checked the other two however nothing came up there. I think someone has bought a batch from Manchester, Edinburgh or even Dundee, not knowing it was deadly," said Diamond. "We will have to go public with this information. At least we can warn the punters about this stuff. I'll get Amy to make an appointment with the local papers, to put a warning out. Not that it will do much good. Addicts will take anything. It's as if they don't care if they live or die," he continued.

"Maybe it would be a good idea to aim it at parents who will be much more afraid for their children."

Two days later, a dire warning from DI Diamond appeared in the papers. He appealed to parents to warn their sons and daughters to be very careful.

We have lost eight young people from three cities in the last six weeks. We do not need or want any more young people to die needlessly.

He hoped it would scare them.

The three ladies saw the funeral notice in the *Times*.

"Thank goodness. At least we can be sure," observed Ursula.

When Maddie arrived, she had two newspapers with her and seemed eager to tell them something.

"Ladies, wait till you hear this," she blurted out, reading the article out.

"The police have issued a warning to all Glasgow addicts to avoid buying drugs from anyone they do not know well. As there is a bad batch going about from which three young men have died in the last three weeks. The names of these men are Ian Reid, Thomas Kelly and James Knox."

"Let's see that," exclaimed Ursula.

They all crowded around Maddie hardly believing what they were seeing.

"My God," shrieked Glenda excitedly, "I can hardly believe our luck. They think he was killed by a bad batch coming from Edinburgh."

"We will never be as lucky again," proclaimed Ursula. "The police are not looking for us, so much as a dealer who has used the wrong mixer in the baggies. Do you think that is correct, Maddie? Am I justified in saying that?"

"You definitely are, Ursula. You've got it in one," replied Maddie.

"We still better wait a few weeks before the next one, Ursula," Glenda added. "As it will take a lot more planning for the next one. You can't depend on our luck holding out any more. Far better to be really well prepared.

"Also, remember, Maddie, there will be a fair amount of tailing involved for you and Ursula. We don't know as much about Shepherd as we did for Thomson and Knox," finished Glenda.

"At the same time, Glenda, we will have to organise your trip to Paris. Are you taking your mum or your sister?" asked Ursula.

"My sister. Mum and Kim are planning one of their trips. I think it's Millport or Oban. Not too sure. They spend each evening planning what to take, where to go. I think they have caught the island-hopping bug," she continued.

"That's enough for now, Maddie. You and I will work out how to tail Shepherd. The usual stuff: where and when. Two weeks will be enough."

"Glenda, you check we have everything we need. Now, home, and a good night's sleep for a change."

To herself, she thought, when I have a spare moment, I'll be having a look-see at Mr Campbell McIntosh.

Chapter 51

As Glenda was not involved with tailing Shepherd, she had been catching up doing a little shopping for Paris. Also, buying Mum a new camera and binoculars for their trip. She had decided to visit her sister, Jane, who was the oldest of the four sisters.

On opening the front door, Jane was all smiles.

"Come in, come in, it's so nice to see you. I must admit, you are looking a wee bit better. Sit down and we'll have a nice cup of tea and a cake. Then tell me all your news. Mum said you were being very good about going to the bereavement class. Well done. It was a hard pill to swallow to lose Ryan. I can see you are on the mend, baby sister, never forget we will always be here for you. Just like old times. I have some good news to tell you. My own wee Emma is going out with a very nice young man. His name is David Thomson and he comes from Knightswood. Nice, eh?" said Jane.

Glenda agreed, however, at the same time, her heart fell to her boots. Hell, she thought, I will have to phone Ursula as soon as. This is an emergency.

"It's been great seeing you, Jane, and I will come back more often in future."

Jane waved her to the car, calling, "Don't be a stranger, Glenda."

So kind. I am so very lucky to have my family, Glenda mused.

When she arrived at the flat, Ursula and Maddie were there with coffee ready. Glenda, of course, was in a bit of a flap.

"Now, sit down, Glenda, drink your coffee and tell us slowly what is wrong," Ursula spoke reassuringly.

"I went to visit my sister, Jane, to catch up on all the news. She told me her daughter, Emma, had started a friendship with a David Thomson. I just knew in my bones he was related to that shit, Thomson. I just knew," she almost sobbed. "After a bit of probing, I found out he is Matt Thomson's nephew. Now, Ursula, I'm all in a lather. What do you ladies think?" she gasped.

"Now first, Glenda, it might not be as bad as you think," protested Ursula. "Yet again, there is not too much we can do about it at this stage. Do not panic. You are in no way connected to Matt Thomson. I repeat, no way, so stop worrying. It is just nerves, you know that." She paused. "I admit, it is a bit of a blow but not serious. No one can trace either you or Maddie to this man. On the other hand, did you ever mention our names to any of your family?"

"No, no, Ursula, I only speak of my two friends, Ellen and Catherine, at the bereavement class. So you are safe. You schooled us well, Ursula."

Ursula nodded.

"Glenda, don't worry. Nothing can come of it. Furthermore, we will take precautions. Ursula and I will do a wee bit of sleuthing and find out how the land lies. Now, settle down. You know we will look after one another. Now, no more panicking," Maddie added.

Ursula, who missed nothing, noted Maddie's kind hand give Glenda a gentle pat. Inwardly, she smiled.

Ursula spent the next week shadowing Emma and the Thomson boy. They appeared to have lots of friends of both sexes. She followed him to work, and golfing with his dad on Saturday morning, thinking to herself that might be a hobby I'll take up when this is all over.

Maddie went to town on Saturday morning, following Emma and her mum shopping, then she had lunch, not too near them, in Marks and Spencer.

Ursula found the Thomson boy to be a nice lad: steady job, lived at home with his parents, one brother, one sister. He had a car and dressed well. He went out to dinner on Saturday evening with Emma. Ursula spied Maddie parked up the street where she had been tailing Emma. Not a lot of drinking was involved. Happily, no drugs. All in all, nice kids, thought Ursula. What most parents wanted for their children. . . decent young people going about an ordinary lifestyle. Very much like her own children had been before Matt Thomson, she reflected.

The following Sunday, Maddie and Ursula were happy to report back to Glenda.

"We found out that everything is fine. There is absolutely no need for worry. No concern at all," Ursula reassured her.

"In fact," continued Maddie, "I think she has met a very nice, stable young man and he has met a girl who is a kindred spirit to himself."

"I wish my son, Simon, had lived long enough to have met such a pleasant young woman," murmured Ursula, choking back a small sob.

They both glanced at her. It was not often she displayed such sorrow. They both reached out and touched her hand gently.

Shaking herself, Ursula said quickly, "Some lunch, ladies, then down to business. First, we must settle on a date. I propose three weeks this coming Saturday. That gives us four weeks to prepare. Does that sound okay with you two?" she asked, looking from one to the other.

"Good for me," answered Glenda. "That means you can book my flight and hotel, Ursula. My sister, Sarah, was over the moon when I mentioned a trip to Paris. *'I've never been to France,'* she said. *'Well, neither have I,'* I said to her. What a treat for us."

"Remember, Glenda, Paris is the city of love, so you had better behave yourself," Maddie teased her.

"That will make this one six weeks from Knox, so it's well spaced out. Any suggestions?" Ursula asked.

"No," they both answered together.

"Maddie, you and I are on tailing duty this week. We know nearly nothing about this Shepherd girl."

"I quite like the dressing up part of tailing," she replied, giving a little wiggle.

They both smiled at her.

"I'm not sure where she goes with friends or family. She is bound to go out to dinner or a club once a week," Maddie explained. "So, it's back to the drawing board for this one."

"Before we go, ladies. Everything is on the drawing board for this one." Her face became more serious. "Also, I want you both to give a bit of serious thought to that lawyer, Campbell McIntsoh. I will never rest till that man is dealt with."

They looked at her. Ursula was determined to pay him back. That's for sure, the thought occurred to them both.

But not a word was spoken.

Chapter 52

Life had been extremely busy for DI Diamond and DS McNeil. The desk in front of them was filled with reports of the other four Glasgow clubs they were looking into. On the pin board were photos of known dealers who supplied most of the staff. Once again, the big boys were absent, most likely in Spain, lolling about their villas or enjoying the sun on a rented yacht somewhere on the Mediterranean Sea.

"The only way we are ever going to catch the big fish is for the law to change on tax evasion," said an exasperated Diamond.

"The problem being, they pay lawyers and accountants mega bucks to make the cash more or less untraceable," answered DS McNeil.

"Meanwhile, we are left with this bloody mess. Three more deaths, two in Edinburgh and one in Glasgow. Reports from the troops suggest no one new is selling. We nicked two of them, however, as usual Andrew, they are all blind, deaf and dumb," Diamond said bitterly.

"I'm going to try something new this time," he said. "I'm going to work with the newspapers when I go public. I will appeal to the mothers and fathers to protect their children from these scumbags. Andrew, that young guy from Edinburgh was only fifteen years old. It's enough to put years on you.

"We will issue them a direct phone number. They do not have to give their names. Only the name of the dealer, then replace the phone," continued Diamond.

"That might just work," agreed McNeil. "Even if we save one young life, it will be worth it."

"I will get in touch with the *Daily Record* and the *Evening Times*. They are always up for a good story. I know if I had a teenager who was taking a wee bit something at the weekend, I sure as hell would give the dealer's name. These guys have been running amok in this town for too long and I think it's time we played them at their own game for a change. Get me three men to man the phones around the clock and remember they only report to either you or me personally," he concluded.

Next day, a meeting took place in Diamond's office with DS McNeil, DI Robert Sawyer, DS Bill Andrews and DS Sandy Lawson in attendance.

DI Diamond took the lead. Now we are all aware of the drug situation, gentlemen. It's getting very dangerous as young people are dying. We already have three men to man the phones. We will have to use everything and everybody to help. It's bad enough, the fights between two rival gangs, but there have been eight stabbings in the last month. Surprisingly, not a single person has seen a thing. Even the buggers who were stabbed. Now, we all have our secret 'helpers'. Use them, scare the bloody hell out of them if you have to. We cannot let this problem escalate any further. Use your men to put the frighteners on the small fry. Word will soon travel up the grapevine." Diamond paused.

"Will we have much help, Sir?" asked Sandy Lawson.

"Yes," replied Diamond. "You will each have two constables to help with research and paperwork. However, you four and your men are a team. A special room is being set up just now with all the equipment you will require."

"What about the cases we are already on, Sir?" Bill Andrews queried.

"They'll be reallocated elsewhere. Don't worry. Word from upstairs is this is given priority. The chief constable wants it stopped and stopped right now. Before it becomes another Manchester or London. There will be no hiding place for them here. Any questions?" he said.

"Not just yet," said Andrews.

"To finish, we meet at the same time, about nine, in room four, each Wednesday. By the way, the name of this operation is *Operation Mayhem*. Hopefully, that's what we will cause amongst the big guys. Thank you, gentlemen," he said, smiling wryly as he stood up to leave the room.

Chapter 53

Ursula took first turn at tailing Allison Shepherd noting when and where she went to work. She'd been moved to the surgical wards, most likely where she could do the least harm, thought Ursula cynically.

Shepherd called in at the supermarket on her way home, next, stopping in Lenzie where she stayed for dinner, calling back as she left, "Bye Mum. Say bye to Dad."

Her mother worked in the local library and her dad was a teacher. Ursula knew this because her mother said, while saying cheerio, that he had an evening class so would be home a little later.

She drove a mini which had seen better days. Maddie had said she was on the lookout for a new car. Might be a useful wee bit of information as she was not a drug addict so that method was out. Also, not diabetic so that was no good.

Maddie took the evenings tailing Shepherd. One wee surprise was she had a driving lesson on the Thursday evening. Puzzled, she wondered why. It was definitely a lesson. Maddie waited on tenterhooks outside the driving school for almost an hour. Shepherd had left her mini so she would be back.

As the school car rounded the corner Maddie heaved a sigh of relief. She had been right after all.

Leaving the car, she said to the instructor, "Thanks so much, Mr Noble, I'll see you on Tuesday at six-thirty," as she returned to her own car.

Maddie was baffled. Why would anybody take lessons when they could already drive? I'll leave that to Ursula to figure out. Better to give her a call, then she is forewarned. Following Shepherd home, she then went home herself.

On Friday, when Ursula arrived at the flat Shepherd and her pals shared, she spied Maddie's car leaving. A quick glance was all they gave one another. It was about eight-thirty before the girls left the flat, dressed for a night out. As she was a taxi driver that evening, she could not follow them into a club or pub. Their taxi arrived. The young women all got in laughing and smiling.

"Mingles, please," said one as Ursula prepared to follow them. They stopped outside a club near Glasgow. As they all left the taxi, Ursula, who was dressed as a driver, with her auburn wig on, could not go in after them. Mingles catered for the young. The music was loud and the thump-thump resounded outside. I must be getting old, she mused. Maddie and Glenda can investigate that side of things, she thought, as she left for home.

At the flat on Sunday, Ursula had coffee ready as they prepared to catch up. Ursula confessed she did not have a great deal to tell.

"Shepherd is in the surgical wards and it's work and home. She does a little shopping, goes to her parents for dinner once a week. Not a lot at all. How about you, Maddie? Did you fare any better? Oh, I might add, I followed the flatmates and Shepherd to a club called Mingles outside Glasgow. But couldn't go in. That's up to you two. You will have to plan very carefully for this one. I have a feeling this one will be much more difficult than the last two," she grumbled.

Maddie agreed. "It's what to do with her that worries me most, Ursula. I cannot understand why anyone who can drive is taking driving lessons. Anyone got any ideas?"

"That's a puzzle," agreed Glenda, "yet there must be a reason. Do you think it might be that the new car she is buying could be a wee bit more upmarket than she is used to driving?"

Ursula exclaimed, "Do you know, Glenda, I think you have hit the nail on the head."

"I always said she is a wee genius," gasped Maddie. "She can now afford something a lot better. And a little more powerful. Most people who get a big car take maybe one or two lessons in it, with the instructor."

"You are right, Glenda," added Maddie. "When I bought this car, it was the first automatic I had driven. My uncle took me out for an hour's lesson. Do you know, I had completely forgotten that."

"That's probably the reason. Well done, Glenda," agreed Ursula. "I think it would be helpful if you two could go to the club this Friday. You will need to be ultra careful, Glenda. Maddie, you've become skilled at becoming a different person so you will do Glenda's makeup or, in fact, a complete makeover, totally different from the real you, Glenda. Also, sit a good distance away from those three and make sure your back is facing Shepherd because it is a risk. We can't have her recognising you as the parent of a former patient, Glenda. However, it must be done as I am not young enough to go to that club," explained Ursula.

"We will go over it very carefully, Ursula. We know not to take any risks," said Maddie.

"Right, we'll leave it at that. Maybe it would be useful if we all put our thinking caps on for this one. As I am doubtful as to doing anything in that club," went on Ursula.

"It depends on how we do it as to when we move," added Maddie.

"We'll say goodnight for now. Hopefully, one of us will get a brainwave," persisted Ursula.

Chapter 54

DI Diamond had been lucky enough to get a fifteen-minute slot on Radio Scotland where he had stressed the need for caution when buying drugs.

"Not to put a fine point on it, the stuff on sale now is particularly dangerous. In fact, to be honest, it is lethal."

"Why, DI Diamond, is that so?" asked Amanda Lewis, the lady interviewer.

"We have had three deaths in Dundee. Three in Edinburgh about six months ago. Then a lull. Now we have another three fatalities in Glasgow. So somebody is selling a bad batch here. Thus, in order to prevent any more unnecessary deaths, we are issuing a severe warning."

"Have they all been from the same mixture, DI Diamond?" Amanda asked.

"Yes, they have," he answered. "Therefore, we know it's the same people selling. One can't prevent addicts from buying. On the other hand, we hope guys who are not dependent and only use for party time will be much more careful who they acquire from in future," Diamond continued.

Amanda asked, "How are they to know who to not buy from?"

"Someone they don't know, maybe with an Edinburgh accent. I surmise these guys are long gone. The stuff has been downloaded onto the local dealers. There is no really sure way, except by not buying. I cannot put it any other way. These boys are dealing out death," he continued.

Miss Lewis nodded in agreement with him. "Thank you so much DI Diamond. I hope you people out there are paying attention to this extremely serious warning," she stated. "Thank you once again, DI Diamond."

"The Glasgow newspapers have done a great job by keeping this matter in the public eye," remarked Diamond.

"They have passed on nearly one hundred names from their phone lines. The warning you gave on the radio would surely frighten the punters. Surely they would learn a lesson from that," answered McNeil. "It will be interesting to compare their list with ours," he went on.

"The news from the clubs is that business is a wee bit slow just now. No wonder," said Diamond. "I think it's a case of rats and sinking ships," he mused.

"They know we mean business and we will close them down if there are any more fatalities. It's as much in their interest as ours to stop these people. Maybe the middlemen have buggered off to Manchester or London. I am hearing from the plain clothes coppers that the streets are not so busy. These guys know that parents will protect their kids by reporting them. I have one friend whose son is now attending a clinic. He is their only child who has previously ignored all their warnings. However, they will report his dealer and he knows it. It's a case of stop now or you could be the next one to die," said McNeil.

"We can compare these two lists then see what that gives us. You just never know." He paused to look at his report.

"To my mind, Sir, it's a case of trying to deter them from smoking cannabis when they are teenagers. They have the mistaken idea that it's fine to smoke a wee bit weed now and again. If the truth be told, if they see their parents smoking some wacky baccy, it must be okay. It's a myth that it is harmless," maintained McNeil. It was the one thing he was very much against.

"You're so right, Andrew," agreed Diamond. "No way it's harmless. It's the first rung on the ladder of addiction. Besides being the street dealers' bread and butter. I read a scientific article somewhere which said that smoking cannabis is doubly dangerous for teens as those years are when the brain is at an important stage of development," Diamond said.

McNeil answered, "I wouldn't be surprised if it was a major cause in the rising cases of suicide in young men. The government would do well to come down a wee bit harder on drug use. The softly, softly approach does not appear to be working. While we are left to clear up the mess every time," he sighed.

"On the other hand, that doesn't help us with our problem. I've called a meeting for our team, Bobby, Bill and Sandy, for ten in the morning. Also, the chief has called a meeting next Tuesday with the heads of Dundee, Edinburgh and Glasgow. It's all-hands-on-deck for a solution. We will have to see what we can come up with." As DI Diamond closed his folder in disgust.

Chapter 55

Maddie and Glenda were taking extra care with their makeovers.

"I can't go as Patsy," said Maddie. "This is an altogether different kind of club from Dundee. More middle class than working class, I would say."

Glenda added, "Nothing like Thomson's club. That was a more male and older clientele. This place is very much for the young. I don't have a good feeling about this one, Maddie. Somehow, we are on the wrong track. Even you and I are too old for this place," she sighed. "Nonetheless, we will follow Ursula's instructions. She wants us to see the lie of the land. I don't think she is quite sure of how and where to do this one. She will know how to proceed when we report back to her," she said as she adjusted her skirt and top, not too short but shorter than she was used to.

"This is a really nice wig, Glenda. I think I will hang onto it afterwards. I love this colour."

"It's ash blonde, Maddie. You suit that shade. Also, you have smashing legs," she said, looking in admiration at her. "I am too small to be glam. I must admit, losing one-and-a-half stone has helped me look a tiny bit better. I can now wear nice tops and slinky trousers for a change," wiggling in front of the mirror. "I'm keeping this gear for Paris," she said.

Maddie smiled at her. "I thought Ursula might use a plan involving that new car. Maybe a tragic accident?"

"Oh, tragic indeed," uttered Glenda with a smirk.

Mingles was busy. Maddie and Glenda found a seat at the back. Maddie went up to the bar and bought two gins and small bottles of mixers. She had a plastic bottle in her bag into which she poured the gin.

"Not a night for a drink, Glenda. Need to keep our wits about us with this lot," she grinned.

Glenda said, "Tonic water is good for us. The last thing we need is to get stopped and breathalysed."

"Too right," answered Maddie.

When Allison Shepherd and her two flatmates appeared, they met up with two more young women who took charge of ordering and buying the drinks.

Maddie could see Glenda was extremely nervous at the sight of them even though Maddie was facing them. They seemed to be enjoying each other's company, speaking animatedly and laughing, with eyes for no one else in the club.

"I thought Ursula said Shepherd would not be here tonight," said Glenda. She could feel her heart throbbing in her chest almost like a drumbeat.

"She most likely changed her mind when she discovered those two were coming," putting her hand, comfortingly, over Glenda's. "Never mind, Glenda, your own mother would never recognise you in your new glitzy outfit." Maddie could see she was like a hen on a hot griddle. I hope this is the only time we have to meet them. It's too much for poor Glenda, she thought. "You know, Glenda, there is no sign of anybody either buying or selling any stuff in this club. I find that unusual. What do you think?"

Glenda was trying to gather her thoughts together before answering.

"I did notice a security man at the door as we came in. That would surely put dealers off. It might be all this police publicity is having an effect. Also, the police must be keeping an eye on street dealers who will be keeping a low profile. Only selling to well-known buyers at local venues."

"I expect you're right, Glenda." Glad to see Glenda was more herself and she had been taking note of the situation in spite of her anxiety. She's a plucky wee soul, mused Maddie.

The girls left about eleven-thirty. Maddie and Glenda soon after. Not much had been learned. Yet you could never tell with Ursula. Just what she could deduce from what they had to tell.

Chapter 56

DI Diamond and DS McNeil met with their colleagues from Edinburgh, DI Sandy Stewart and DS Peter Gilmore, on Tuesday morning. After introductions, the meeting opened with both sides giving account of how many young men had lost their lives. It was far more serious than it had first appeared.

DI Stewart explained, "If we count the fatalities from Edinburgh, Dundee, Glasgow and small towns, we have twenty-three deaths in all. We feel there are new dealers in Edinburgh. Our usual informants seem to be very wary of giving any information to coppers who know them well."

DS Peter Gilmore continued, "It may well be that the local guys just don't know who the big guys are buying from. They are all missing. . . gone off to Spain or wherever they go."

DI Stewart agreed and continued, "We thought at first it was hooligans from Manchester who were trying to muscle in, however, we have now come to the conclusion that there are bigger fish in this mixture."

Peter Gilmore spoke, "Maybe the London mob. If that's the case we need to pool our resources and every town in Scotland has to have a small select team working together with us three large towns to stamp out these guys. The last thing we want is for this problem to escalate," he continued.

"I agree," DI Diamond answered, "however, the last three or four deaths have not been from the usual goof balls. Word from the lab is fifty percent heroin, not the usual twenty-five percent plus they are not using sugar, bicarbonate of soda or even chalk. Cheapest rubbish they have. The terrifying thing about two Glasgow deaths were a mixture of ecstasy, the party drug, and heroin, a death sentence for sure. Someone does not know what they are doing here. In my opinion, they have an under-qualified chemist working for them. If there are any more deaths from this mixture I expect to find this trainee chemist asleep in the woods. He is costing too much money, and we can, through time, trace it back to a single source," finished Diamond.

"Frankly," said DS McNeil, "these people do not take any prisoners. The top brass have high-priced briefs. It only takes one phone call and we will find our chemist in the canal or the woods."

"Yeah, they will do away with him. We find him, with all the evidence on him. They have given us the culprit. They must think we came up the Clyde on a banana boat to think we would fall for that one," maintained Diamond. "On the other hand, it may create a fall in the drug deaths for a while as they sort themselves out. I foresee a few stabbings or shootings amongst the hierarchy before this is finished."

"Maybe it might pay us to take a back seat, leaving them to fight it out for a while. Then we can step in and pick up the pieces," said McNeil.

DI Diamond smiled at that, remarking, "If we do not all keep hammering away at this problem, get the tiddlers off the streets, it might make our cities too hot to handle. We need more coppers going into schools to educate our kids to show them that drugs are for mugs."

"Well, gentlemen, thank you for coming. Next week, I meet with the Dundee team. We will make Glasgow central to all three cities. That way everybody is kept informed."

They all closed their folders; the meeting had been successful. More importantly, in their eyes, war had been declared.

Chapter 57

The Daily Record headline read,

Child run down in East End of Glasgow.

It was intended to horrify and it did. The story continued to tell of an innocent little girl walking home from school along the pavement when a driver, losing control of her car, mounted the pavement, striking Emma Steel, aged seven. The child was killed instantly.

Her father, when interviewed, said, "Our Emma was only minutes from home. There is a twenty mile-an-hour limit where she was walking," he maintained. "Far too many drivers ignore the rule. Only parents of the pupils pay any heed to the signs. My wife and I are distraught. Emma was our only child."

The Record went on to say the slaughter on our roads was a national disgrace.

Ursula and Maddie were reading this report when Glenda entered the flat.

"I hope the woman driver of that car was not over the limit," said Ursula, "or the *Record* will make a banquet of it."

"It's a bloody nightmare," agreed Maddie. "No one appears to care about our children. Thoughtless, stupid swines that they are. I think it will be a good thing is the *Record* does run with it," she ranted.

"The only worry I would have is if the paper did a little more research on older cases and discover our two miscreants, Knox and Thomson, and their happy endings," she paused, looking back at them both with a serious glance. "Remember, newspapers are like policemen. They do not put events down to coincidence or karma. They deal in facts. Patience, ladies, we will bide our time, it's wait and see time for us," she finished.

Next day's *Record* had pictures plus a two-page spread. No way was this story going to bed any time soon.

Their worst fears were realised the following week when the *Record* took up the story once again. The woman driver, Mrs Kate Barrie, age forty-two, had been well over the limit, thus had been charged. The paper took it even further, telling its readers that on weekdays, thirty percent of road accidents are caused by drivers over the limit while at weekends, the figure increases to fifty-two percent. Another dreadful disclosure was the fact that you could pay a lawyer a great deal of money to have the charge reduced with no mention of any fatality having occurred.

Of course, no names were disclosed. While on the other hand, given time, they just might be.

The three ladies looked at one another, dumbstruck.

"My heavens," exclaimed Ursula. "These guys are really playing hardball," she went on.

Maddie said, "That's just what we need. Someone who will fight in our corner for a change. What about this nasty wee nugget on the next page?" She read it out, almost with glee.

"The *Record's* advice for anyone who has had an accident while over the limit, or caused an injury or even a fatality, is to go online shopping where you will be spoilt for choice."

When asked why the police cannot do more for this dreadful state of affairs, DI Diamond replied, "While we are most sympathetic, the police can only work within the law, as it stands now. In response to the overwhelming feedback from *Daily Record* readers, we have decided to run a competition. We want to find a slogan making the public much more aware of the dangers of driving while under the influence of alcohol.

The competition drew hundreds of entries. It was the biggest story for years. However, only two people wrote in to ask why they didn't change the law? It's only logical after all. But that didn't go anywhere.

Maddie added, "Why doesn't some bright young journalist, out to make a name for themselves, take up this angle. People know drivers only pay lip service to the drink regulations. What the hell can we do, they ask."

"Change will come some day," retorted Ursula. "When people are sick to death of scraping our precious children off the roads like so much roadkill," she said with as much sorrow as bitterness.

Chapter 58

Ursula was at home finishing her housework, not that there was much to do. Lately, she found herself going over and over all they had done, searching in her mind for mistakes. The fear of being caught was an ever present danger. Not even to be contemplated. She worried about her ladies more than herself. They were young. When this was over, they could turn their lives around. She dismissed these negative fears as ill-conceived rubbish, scolding herself. Better to be thinking of this next assignment: that Shepherd woman.

As far as she could see, it was far more difficult. Taking much more careful planning than the last two. Also, Maddie was in charge of the plan for that lawyer. A devious man, a parasite, despicable in every way. She could feel black hatred welling up inside her. No, no, don't go there. Her mother would say the only way someone can hurt you is if you let them.

She would get ready to meet her girls. I should have not watched that memorial programme. Thinking to herself, every day for the rest of my life is memorial day. She knew in her heart she would never get over it.

She shook herself, saying out loud, "Onwards and upwards."

At the flat, she busied herself making lunch for Glenda and Maddie. Her mood lightened.

"When do you think I should book my break, Ursula?" asked Glenda.

"I would look at three weeks come Saturday, dear but first, I would like to hear about the club. Mingles, is it?" she asked.

"Yes," answered Maddie. "It is a lot different from the Thomson one. More upmarket. Also a much younger crowd. The thing was, Ursula, there was no sign of anyone buying or selling stuff. We thought it was on account of a higher police presence and more publicity.

"If you think using drugs is a bad idea, I think we should drop the club from our plans."

Both ladies gave each other a knowing glance.

"Glenda, what are your thoughts on that?" asked Ursula.

"To be honest, Ursula, I had my doubts about this one. It is far more difficult than the last two. A lot more planning and detail is needed."

"She is not just a pretty face, Ursula, is she?" said Maddie.

Ursula said, "I will think it over girls. That new car sounds like a good idea to me. Not an accident, as I have plans for another person to be involved in a car accident.

"So, get your thinking cap on, Maddie. What I need is a lot more information about that new car. Make, model, and where she will keep it. In a garage, lock-up or surely not in the street. You and I will follow her on the next two lessons. I have a feeling they will be the last two."

"Glenda, you will, as near as possible, arrange Mum and Kim's trip for the date I gave you. I will get your tickets for you and your sister and also book your hotel in Paris. Your spending money is in the drawer in the bedroom."

Glenda raised her hand in protest.

"Glenda, it's Simon's money, for *our* use, so no more, please."

"About this lawyer," said Maddie. "Anyone have any good ideas?"

"I have," said Ursula. "Leave it with me. Something for the three of us to do together."

Glenda and Maddie looked at her but said nothing.

"I think he is a barrister not a lawyer because he works in the courtroom," Glenda informed them.

"I could think of a name for him beginning with a 'B' and it's not barrister," snorted Maddie. "What's his name anyway?"

"Campbell McIntosh," replied Ursula. "I, for one, will never forget it.

"Now, that's it, ladies, we have a lot to think about this week as we have no concise plan yet. So we are open to suggestions.

"Are you okay, Glenda?"

"Yes, Ursula, I have a bit of shopping to do. Is there anything you two need for trailing? Also, are we up to date with gloves and these white suits?"

"So far, fine, Glenda," said Maddie.

"My mother is redecorating in new colours. So, I would be as well out of her way," she smiled.

"Glenda, could you get me another wig in a dingy brown for a taxi driver?"

"No bother," replied Glenda, scribbling in her note pad.

Chapter 59

DI Diamond contacted the *Record* newspaper requesting an interview with one of their editors, which was granted the following morning.

He and McNeil met with a Mr Eric Liddle.

"I am DI Diamond and this is my colleague, DS McNeil. I was hoping you could give us a little more help, Mr Liddle?"

"It's Eric, DI Diamond. How can I be of assistance to you gentlemen?"

"We would like you to do an article appealing to parents who have young people who are using drugs, even if they only suspect them of buying at the weekend," Diamond said.

McNeil went on, "We will issue a phone number which will be manned twenty-four hours. Moreover, stress they do not have to give their names. Only the dealer's name and where they are selling. We will deal with the rest."

Diamond went on, "After all, over twenty young people have died nationwide so far."

Eric Liddle was more than pleased to help.

"No bother, I'll get on to it immediately. It could be any one of us whose children are involved in this. This problem appears to be escalating. Is there a reason for this?"

"Yes indeed," replied McNeil. The profits they make from drugs is colossal. In addition, the big boys rule over the tiddlers with a rod of iron, literally."

Liddle looked from one policeman to the other, aghast.

"Heavens, I don't envy you your problems. I'll get my end of things organised as soon as. Will I phone each evening with any information I may have?"

"That will be most helpful, Eric. We will let you get on now and thank you once again."

Liddle led them towards the staircase where they shook hands.

"Well, that went better than I thought," said Diamond.

DS McNeil conceded, "One, it helps us and two, it keeps his story going for a while longer."

At the Mayhem meeting a week later, everyone had quite a bit to contribute.

DI Diamond informed them about his meeting with Eric, also telling them, "The Glasgow newspapers have done a grand job by keeping this matter in the public eye. What's more, the winner of the caption competition was awarded one hundred pounds prize money and his picture in the *Record*. It was:

Don't be a cad

Call for a cab,"

he declared.

"That's neat," grinned McNeil. "Also they have passed on nine names from Glasgow and surrounding areas."

"Might be interesting to compare our names to any the *Record* has. Word on the street is business is slow. The reason is simple. The three towns are awash with coppers. Myself, I think it's a case of rats and sinking ships," Diamond voiced. "What about your lot, Sandy?"

"We caught two dealers selling. Not at the school gates but fairly near. Nabbed by uniformed coppers. These guys are becoming desperate for business," replied Sandy. "Any luck with you, Bobby?" he asked DI Sawyers.

"There is a distinct element of fear in Edinburgh. Our guys have been putting the frighteners on the small fry. They know for sure we are after them, big time. We have caught three dealers whose names are also on the *Record's* list. Besides, the big boys have retreated to their lairs in Spain or wherever," added Sawyers. "Did you get any word back from your lab as to what the hell they are mixing?" he asked.

"They reckon there is a wee bitty ketamine in with the heroin. As we all know, that is a sure death sentence. What's more, if they are caught it will be a much harsher sentence."

"That's bound to earn them a wee holiday at her Majesty's pleasure," added DI Andrews wryly. "Come down really hard on these pests. As my old boss used to say, remember ABC: *Assume nothing, Believe no one, Check everything.*

"The bosses have a lot more to lose than the dealers. Houses, cash and jewellery. Tax evasion is the thing that scares them most. Plus, they can't put cash into the bank. What we need, gentlemen, is one or two suppliers to fall into our net."

"That's about it for today. See you all in a couple of weeks as we all have more than enough to contend with," said Diamond. "Thank you very much, gentlemen," as he put his notes into a large folder. He finished, "Now for a light lunch."

Chapter 60

Maddie and Ursula were racking their brains to think of a way to deal with Shepherd.

"Tell you what, Ursula," said Maddie, "why don't I tail her tonight? It's not a club night and what's more, I don't think, in her case, drugs are a good idea, do you? Also, those driving lessons are driving me crazy, I tell you. Why? Why? I keep asking myself."

"I think you're right, Maddie. She is a doctor after all and will be aware of drugs. Also, I don't want Glenda involved in this one."

I agree, Ursula. She very nearly lost the plot the other night at that club. To see and hear that girl's nearness was too much. So we will leave her out of this one."

Glenda arrived ten minutes later.

"Hallo ladies, sorry to be late. I was held back at work."

"No bother, Glenda," they both said.

"Here is a nice cuppa," said Maddie, setting the cup down beside her.

"Glenda, have you thought any more about your trip yet? Are you still taking your sister?" Ursula asked her.

"Yes. We're off to Paris and Mum and Kim will go to Millport. But, Paris indeed, it's unbelievable. Me, in Paris!

"First, though ladies, I'm still worried about that problem with my niece, Emma. She's going out with Matt Thomson's nephew, David, if you remember, and I don't know what to do. I was at my sister, Jane's on Sunday. They were so pleased to see me and commented on how much better I looked. It was just like old times, great. Then she was talking about Emma and David again. I'm all in a lather about it. What should I do?"

"Now, Glenda," said Maddie. "Stop worrying. There is not much we can do. There's no way you are connected to Matt Thomson. I repeat, no way! There is *no* link between you and him. Did you ever mention our names?"

"No," said Glenda. "You are Ethel and Ursula is Catherine, my friends at the class," she conceded.

"Glenda, no more worrying. We will take precautions. Maddie and I will do a bit of sleuthing. Now, settle down. You know we all look after one another," Ursula added.

Chapter 61

Maddie thanked her lucky stars she was early at Shepherd's flat. Sitting well down in her car seat as she watched Mr Noble, the instructor, arrive and ring the bell.

Shepherd came out all smiles. "Halloo," she said. "Are we going to the dealer's tonight?"

"Yes," he replied. "We pick up your new car at six-thirty. Are you all prepared now?"

Shepherd nodded.

They both got into the man's vehicle. For the life of her, Maddie could not think why. Then, there was no sign of her mini in the street.

It soon dawned on her. She followed them via the back roads to a showroom in Bishopbriggs which they both entered, leaving his car around the back.

Maddie's hands were clammy as she clutched the steering wheel of her own car. Most likely buying herself a new car. Shepherd and Mr Noble were in the showroom for about thirty minutes. Maddie could see them through a large plate glass window. A smart young salesman sat beside the instructor and Shepherd. They seemed to be smiling and laughing. Papers were being signed. The salesman shook hands with them as he led them through a back door.

Maddie moved her car further along the street so no matter which way they turned she would be able to tail them.

Suddenly, as if from nowhere, a very trendy small black car zoomed from the showroom car park. Mr Noble was driving while Shepherd was in the passenger seat.

"What the hell!" exclaimed Maddie out loud. Well, well, wait till I get this news to Ursula, she mused. She hurried to catch up with them as they headed for the quieter streets in

Springburn. Maddie remembered it was a favourite place for instructors to take learners to do three-point turns and parallel parking. At the same time, not too far from the test centre. Parking somewhere not too far away, she took out her phone and an A4 notepad looking for all the world as if she was catching up with the day's work. In fact, she was taking notes as she watched them. They parked just a little way down the street. He appeared to be explaining something to her. Next thing, the roof opened right back. She wrote in her pad: *Mazda MX5. Retractable hardtop.* They changed seats while Mr Noble taught her the controls, practising how to open and close the hood. Then it was the windows' turn to be opened and closed.

Very posh, thought Maddie. Just the car for her. After a practice, Shepherd started the car and moved off quite slowly at first, then when she was maybe a little more confident, they drove for about twenty minutes round the streets. Next, they made for the showroom where the instructor collected his own car. She stayed behind him till they arrived near her flat, the next street, in fact, where there was a little row of lock-ups. She drove into the last one.

Mr Nobel said, "Now, only one more lesson and you are on your own. You seem to be pretty sure of yourself."

Shepherd smiled, saying, "To be honest, it was love at first sight. I just had to have it. You know how it is, don't you?"

"Now, be careful this week. Stay on the quiet roads and I will check on you, Friday. Okay?"

Maddie stayed at the end of the road till they both left. At the same time, she noticed two lock-ups were empty. With a notice on the first one, *To Let*. Interesting, she thought, might be a useful thing for Ursula to know. It's been a hard day's night, however, a lot of beneficial information for Ursula to work around.

At that, she made for home, shower, PJs and bed.

Chapter 62

Ursula had been a wee bit down this week. It had been Simon's birthday so it was understandable. Consequently, she was looking forward to meeting the ladies. Glenda was first to arrive.

"Hi Ursula. I have quite a few bits and bobs for the bedroom. Two new wigs which are a tiny bit different, let's say a little more upmarket, so to speak."

"They look really nice, Glenda. We will get so used to wearing these wigs to look glam we won't be able to stop when this is all over," she laughed.

They both turned at the sound of the door opening as Maddie entered.

"Hallo ladies, I do hope the kettle is on as I am parched," she joked.

"Everything is ready, chicken sandwiches and a fresh cream cake to follow," said Ursula.

"You are a gem, Ursula," Maddie said as they all took a seat.

"We have quite a bit to get through today. Glenda, have you managed to organise your mum and Kim's trip? Is it still to Millport?"

Glenda replied, "Everything is ready. All we need is a firm date, then it's only a matter of confirming the booking. Also, will you be booking the flight and hotel?"

"Yes, that is all in hand. Also, I put your spending money and cash for expenses in the bottom drawer in the bedroom." She raised her hand to stop Glenda's protests. "Now, Glenda, you know all expenses come out of Simon's money. I want you and your sister to have a really nice time. Paris is wonderful. I know you will worry when you are away. I did. You have had little enough fun so far in your life, so enjoy."

"That sounds fine," replied Glenda. "If I have a week's notice of when you two go that should be enough."

"This week, ladies, I will be doing a little sleuthing of David Thomson and your niece, Emma. Better to know how the land lies. We can't take any risks or be caught napping. So that's me this week."

They sipped at the fresh coffee Glenda had made.

"This Shepherd woman appears to be a real puzzle. Maddie, you think clubs and drugs are a no go?"

"Yes, I do, Ursula, because she is a doctor and may well suss that out. Better still, I followed her two nights ago. She went with her driving instructor to Bishopbriggs where she bought a new car, well, new to her. I surmise she has sold the mini in part exchange for this one."

Glenda blurted out, "Maybe she could have a wee accident."

Ursula replied, "No, Glenda. We can't let her have a wee accident as I intend Campbell McIntosh to have a big accident when the time comes."

Both ladies looked at each other, however, said nothing.

Maddie continued, "This car is a Mazda MX5. She will be the envy of all her friends and flatmates, I expect. A retractable hardtop if you please, low-slung, and it has those bucket seats. I imagine it would not be long before you had a sore back," Maddie went on.

"Well, they do say you may as well be dead as out of fashion," Glenda sniffed.

"To continue, she drove it to a quiet street in Springburn where she practised, under the instructor's supervision, using the controls. Seems to be buttons for this, buttons for that. Also, opening the top, the windows and the roof appears to be connected in some way, I'm not sure.

"She then drove back to the dealer's to collect his car then they both went back to the street next to her flat. There is a row of lockups where she put the new car inside. As he left, he called out, *'See you Thursday, remember that's the last lesson'*. I did notice, Ursula, there were two more lockups for rent. Might be a handy wee place to store Simon's car while pretending it's mine."

"That's a lot of good information, Maddie. You have given me lots to think about. As you were talking, I had a glimmer of light flashing into my mind. But not for her, might need it later.

"By the way, can you give me the number of those lockups. I'll get on to them in the morning. Glenda, is there any chance you can have a look-see at Campbell McIntosh and his wife? I have a sneaking suspicion we will need a lot of background stuff on him," added Ursula.

"Happy to help, Ursula, as I am not too busy this week. Mum and Kim are very busy with plans for their next adventure. They have given me a list of what they need," she laughed.

"Well, that's us for today, ladies. Thanks for everything, and that phone number, Maddie."

Chapter 63

Ursula and Maddie took turns in tailing Shepherd. In the flat, they had coffee then decided to brainstorm.

"What do you think, Maddie?" asked Ursula. "Any brilliant ideas come to you yet?"

"Not a one so far. You always advise us to take no risks but this one is different. I have my car around the corner from her lockup. You have put Simon's car in our lockup. So she may see me passing. Not too sure if I should nod or smile. The strange thing is she sits in her car putting the top back and forward, however, does not drive away. What do you make of that?"

"Not sure. Maybe she has had a drink and knows not to drive but gets some kind of kick from just sitting there. I hope you have on your black wig when you are passing her."

"I have also skintight leggings and a sparkly top. To make matters worse I have a joint in my hand. This time, Ursula, I may have to take a risk. It's the only way. I've looked at it from every angle and nothing works. She may invite me to go to the club with her flatmates. To be honest, my own mother would never know me in my new get-up. Now, what is your honest opinion?"

"I don't think putting a tube from the exhaust into the window is a good idea. These forensic people are far too good nowadays. I read that book you recommended by Kate Bendelow. She tells you what to avoid like fingerprints and hairs. Also DNA," said Ursula.

"I will need to become her wee pal. We could come home from the club, have a drink in her car while she plays with the windows and the top. We could have a right laugh, maybe drop a bit something into her drink, making her drowsy. In fact, I have an idea," added Maddie. "You know these small portable BBQ things you can cook on. I read somewhere that they give off the same gas, carbon monoxide, as car exhaust. That's why you must use them outside and not in an enclosed space. A closed lockup, for example. She would need to be sleepy before I leave. Maybe light it or drop a match into it before I close the door."

"That might work, Maddie. It's a hell of a risk and we would need to work it out properly, down to the very last minute and detail," Ursula continued.

"The thing is, Ursula, the night Glenda and I did Thomson, it was just as scary. We were both terrified. Every bit of our bodies was hands and knees shaking and hearts hammering against our ribs. I have never been so aware of the organs inside my body. This time it is not too much different, is it?" she asked.

"Well, put like that, not really. On the other hand, this is just a rough outline of a plan. We must both work on it. It is imperative that it is as perfect as we can make it," conceded Ursula.

"I agree," said Maddie. "You do the Thursday this week. She will be out on her last lesson. I will walk out past her each evening as if I am going home to my flat around the corner. I will do the smiles and nods. On the last night, I will stop to admire her car. That should attract her attention."

"That sounds good but take your time. Go slowly, Maddie."

"I could act dumb, asking daft questions. How does it work? Ooh, that's clever, so neat. Do you just have to press the buttons? How does the top roll back? I will soon be her bestie. Her type just love to feel superior to everyone else. You've met them before, Ursula, at school, at college, even at work."

"I think you're right, Maddie. I can just see you playing that game. You can be so naughty you know."

"I learned quite a bit in Dundee, just watching other people," Maddie added.

"I think we've done enough tonight. Lots to think about. I need this as sleep does not come so easily since I lost my Simon."

Maddie said nothing but put a consoling hand on Ursula's arm.

Shaking herself out of her misery, Ursula smiled.

"Home for us both. I have Primary Three in the morning; they would cheer anybody up," she continued.

"I am on early, very early tomorrow. A really busy ward too."

They both made for the door.

"Goodnight, Maddie."

"Goodnight, Ursula."

Chapter 64

The following fortnight was mostly taken up by Ursula shadowing Emma, Glenda's niece, who worked in an accountant's, nine to five, in town. After work, she walked up to Buchanan Bus Station accompanied by two young ladies who worked beside her. Ursula quite enjoyed the stroll up to the bus stop mingling with the crowds. As she waited outside her house, Emma came out dressed in casual gear. She followed her to the local gym where she stayed an hour or so. Tuesday evening, she stayed at home all evening. Wednesday, David called about six-thirty. They both were smiling as they linked arms, making their way to the cinema.

David appeared to be a nice lad, with a steady job, who owned a car and dressed well. He lived at home and, like Emma, with his parents.

Saturday afternoon, Emma went into town shopping with her mother while in the evening, they were joined by two other couples similar to themselves, for dinner and then on to a club. Sunday morning, David, joined by his father, went to the golf club.

The six friends met at the gym on Sunday evening to play tennis or badminton.

Meeting the ladies on Sunday evening, Ursula could see Glenda had been fretting about her niece.

"Glenda, you have no need for any further stress or worry. Not a lot of drinking was involved with them or their friends. They appear to be nice kids going about a healthy, orderly lifestyle. What's more, to my mind, she has met a pleasant, stable young man. At the same time, he has found a kindred spirit. I only wish my son, Simon, had lived long enough to have met such a charming young woman." She choked back a small sob.

They both glanced at her. It wasn't often she displayed such sorrow. They reached out and gently touched her arm.

Shaking herself, Ursula said quickly, "Some lunch, girls, then down to business. Firstly, we must settle on a date. I propose three weeks this coming Saturday, giving us over three weeks to prepare." Looking from one to the other, she added, "How does that sound to you both?"

They nodded in agreement. Lunch was soup and a quiche. Over coffee, Ursula asked Maddie, "Are you getting anywhere with this Shepherd woman?"

"Well, I am in a way but it all depends on you. I know you said no risks but this one cannot be done without an element of risk."

Ursula raised her hand in protest.

"Maddie, I said no unnecessary risks. However, tell me your plan then we will see from there."

"Honestly, this is the most frustrating thing I have ever done. I seem to be eliminating plans rather than making them." She let out a sigh. "I will have to risk meeting her face-to-face. On the other hand, I will do a complete makeover for this one. Make myself a little older in fact. What about long, straight jet-black hair this time? Glenda, can I leave that with you?"

"No bother, Maddie," replied Glenda.

"Ursula, will you see to renting the last lockup in the row where she keeps her car? We could keep Simon's car in there and pretend it is mine giving me an excuse to pass her lockup. Also we will need false number plates for that one."

"Remember, you will have to park your own car in the next street," said Glenda.

"I will need two weeks to become best buddies with her. Lots of smiles and nods. Admire her new car, ask how it works. Perfect my acting skills. How does the roof roll back? Oh, that's really neat," teased Maddie, rolling her eyes up.

"You can be a devil at times, Maddie," said Glenda. "I can just see you having fun with it."

"We'll leave it with you, Maddie. Remember, as little risk as possible. This is a brief outline. You will have to perfect it," said Ursula. "Now Glenda, how did you get on this week?"

"I did fine. As you know, I caught up with the shopping. Not much to do. Did you need anything, Ursula?"

"Not really. I'll let you know if I do."

"Nobody in my house has any time for me. They are already planning their next adventure. They seem to be having such good fun planning. They sit at the table, all their books spread out. They are going to need warmer jackets and cardigans. Also walking boots, my mum said. You would think they were going to the moon, Ursula.

"And Kim said, *'I have our notebooks, Gran, and pens, to make a nature book. My teacher says to paste pictures in, also leaves can be stuck in like stamps.'* And she wants to know if there will be seals up there too. She's full of it. Mum told her, *'I think we will, sweetie.'* She also explained to her that there is a nice long front at Millport and told her you can hire bikes. And that Mrs Green, who goes to the old folks with her, says there is a great fish and chip restaurant near the bike shop. Not only that, you'll never guess, my mum has bought a pair of warm trousers. She's never worn trousers in her life. I told her they look really nice. She said Mrs Green suggested she got a pair and told her they are very comfortable. Do you know what Mum said, Ursula?"

Ursula smiled with encouragement, enjoying Glenda's enthusiasm.

"She said, *'What your father would say, I just don't know.'*" Glenda laughed. "I'm that pleased for her, ladies. So, this week, I am an added extra. I must admit, it is so nice to see them both so happy. I thought when we lost Ryan those two would never smile again."

"Well," said Ursula, "I think that's us for this week. Lots to think about. Everybody will help with this one. All ideas will be most welcome," she finished.

Chapter 65

Inspector Diamond had been extremely busy of late. There had been a great deal of interaction between two rival Glasgow gangs. Most likely over drugs. Four stabbings, two quite serious but so far, no fatalities. Of course, with these guys, one could never tell. There were always fights however things appeared to be escalating. In a shrinking market there was always trouble. It was only a matter of time before the first body was found in a dark alley. It made no difference how many coppers were on the streets. It was a foregone conclusion. As long as they were establishing top dog it would continue. In this game the profits were too high not to try. He heaved a heavy sigh.

DS Andrew McNeil came in carrying a large folder.

"Morning, Sir, could you sign this lot for me please?"

As Diamond opened the folder and started signing, he asked, "How are things at your end, Andrew?"

"To be quite honest, Sir, you can almost smell the atmosphere on the streets. Something is brewing which will end in trouble. Also, the big boys are conspicuous by their absence. Both Sullivan and Stewart are in in their dark corners plotting like hell against one another while their men appear to be watching and waiting, for what, is anybody's guess."

"I hope it's only our local gangsters in the fray. God forbid, Manchester or London mobsters trying to muscle in on that," mused John.

"Hell's bells, that would be trouble we can do without. Our guys on the streets tell me no one will utter a word," Andrew continued.

"Probably scared stiff," said Diamond, "we will have to keep a very careful eye on the whole situation, wait and see. What about this bad batch situation? Have you heard anything more?" the DI asked.

"Not yet. Things are quiet just now on that front. Personally, I think there is an element of fear amongst the addicts. One reason being, the newspapers are making such a fuss about drugs, giving dire warnings at the same time appealing to parents. Which seems to be working. But the dealers will still have some of the bad batch which they will have to get rid of at some point," Andrews replied.

"Oh, I agree with you there. They will offload it onto some first timers no doubt. These guys are vicious. Money is the god in this game. We will have to crack down on them when this drugs war is over, Andrew," said Diamond.

"Yes Sir," agreed Andrew.

Chapter 66

Maddie spent quite a bit of time surveying the area between Shepherd's flat and the small row of lockups. Parking Simon's car in the end locker, or Locker Two, as she renamed it. Then strolling leisurely past Shepherd's lockup. The first evening, she was sitting in the driver's seat; loud music was playing as she fiddled with the controls. Maddie just looked in. The next evening, the car was outside in the front. Twice, she just said 'Hallo' and walked on. Take it easy, she told herself. Next night, Shepherd was polishing the already gleaming car. Again, just a 'Hallo'. The next time she stopped to look as if admiring the little car.

"That's a lovely wee car," said Maddie. "What kind is it?"

"It's a Mazda MX5," came the answer.

"I see the roof opens up. It's real fancy," agreed Maddie. "Is it harder to drive than an ordinary car?" she said naively.

"Actually, it's a hardtop with a retractable hood," corrected Shepherd. "I've only had it a few weeks. It's my pride and joy," she said proudly. "All my friends are absolutely green with envy. No, it's not harder to drive but a little different. I'm slowly getting used to the controls and buttons. Also, the sound system is fab. However, like everything else, it will take time."

"I think it's a wee beauty," Maddie replied, looking admiringly at the shiny car. "I need to hurry home for my dinner now. By the way, my name is Elizabeth Forbes. Most people call me Beth. I've not long moved here," she went on. "Bye," she said as she made her way to her own car in the next street.

"My name is Allison," was the reply. "Nice to meet you. Most likely see you again if you're passing by." She turned away to her car.

Well, at least contact has been made, she thought. Now to put pen to paper and work out some kind of feasible plan.

After a week and a half, they were becoming quite friendly.

Allison asked Maddie as she passed by, "Would you like to have a seat in it? The seats are a little low but really comfy."

"Would I, yes please," she replied eagerly.

As Maddie seated herself, Allison put on some music. Sitting there, they both enjoyed Gloria Gaynor's *I will survive* amongst other friendly stuff.

"No need to go out," declared Maddie. "You could have a sing-song here in complete comfort," she laughed.

"That's a fact," agreed Shepherd. "I'll need to show you how the controls work sometime," she said.

"That would be great but right now, I'll head home for dinner." Saying goodnight and giving her new pal a cheery wave, she made her way home.

Later, at home, Maddie sat down to do some serious thinking. Tell you what, she thought, I'll do what I used to do before a stiff exam. And taking a large writing pad, she inserted the heading, *Checklist one to six*. Go over every aspect of this. Show it to Ursula, leaving three empty lines for her to fill in her comments or corrections. That way we are less likely to make mistakes.

Glenda will help with the wigs and outfits and gloves, shoes and tracksuits. She is really good at that side of things. She will also be in charge of the rota for transport. Number plates and whose car goes where.

Feeling much better and much more in control of the situation, she took herself off to bed. Sleep, of course, never came easy and she forced herself to turn her mind off.

Her last conscious thought was the smiling face of Sophie. Her bright, shining girl who she had had for such a little time.

Chapter 67

Going over Maddie's checklist, the ladies did a kind of brainstorming exercise. Glenda, betraying how anxious she was, turned to Maddie.

"Please don't take any silly risks. It's not worth it," she pleaded.

"I won't. Now, don't worry. The biggest risk was meeting her face-to-face and now that's over. I was almost unrecognisable in that black wig. Also, I looked a stone heavier in that outfit."

Looking relieved, Glenda continued, "Now to the cars. I suggest you move your car further away and leave a good space in front for Ursula to park her car. I will have false plates on yours and Simon's." She paused to look over her notes.

"Simon's car will already be in lockup two. The old plates are in the boot. You will need to change them back on your way back to the flat. We need to take these precautions. Better to be safe. Also, we need an extra key for Ursula. She will need to hide in it."

"No worries, Glenda. I have a key to Simon's car," replied Ursula.

"Sorry to keep harping on but it is important to change plates. There are bloody cameras all over the place. I advise you both to have something to do in the waiting time, a crossword might be useful. Be extremely careful. You both know the drill, heart hammering, knees knocking, sweat trickling down your back. So be prepared, practise slow breathing, remember when we were in labour, girls.

"First, when you are with Shepherd, doing your sing-song. Again, when you have finished, you will both have to wait until things go quiet. Ursula's car will be parked behind your car and she will drive it home after the event.

"You, Maddie, will drive Simon's car back to the flat. Remember to change the number plates before you leave the lockup. You can work out between you how to get your own car back." She paused, looking down the list, then went on, "Your outfit and black wig, you leave in Simon's car. I think I have gone over everything." She paused again, seeing it all in her mind.

"That sounds fine, Glenda, thank you," answered Ursula. "Maddie, do you have your plan finished, or near enough finished as I will have to follow you as far as I can?"

"Well," replied Maddie, "I will need the rest of the week to become best buddies. Also, I intend to bring a bottle of gin in my bag to help the party along. Will you two point out any glaring mistakes or anything you feel is a little chancy?"

"Yes," replied Ursula, "I'm jotting down as I go along."

"Sure thing, Maddie," added Glenda.

"She may invite me to Mingles on the Saturday. I feel it would set the seal on being a buddy. However, no way can I afford to meet the flatmates. Need an excuse, going out with my cousin. Maybe we can meet at the car after our nights out? Perhaps have a wee sing-song? With a bit of luck, she will agree," she finished.

"So far, so good," replied Ursula. "You will have to play it by ear for the rest as so much depends on her doing what we need to her do."

"Hell, you would need to be a Philadelphia lawyer to work it all out," continued Maddie, reading her notes to see what she had missed.

"Another thing, ladies, I almost forgot, as I was in her car the other evening, I noticed that portable BBQ set in the corner. It might prove useful as I mentioned to you before, Ursula. Good as a back-up plan."

"My, my," observed Glenda, might be a good idea to accidentally drop a lighted match in as you sneak out."

"Exactly, Glenda. We'll leave it up to you, Maddie," added Ursula.

"Always grateful for all suggestions you two come up with," answered Maddie.

"Can I change my mind, Maddie? Better not drop a match in as they can get DNA from it. I read that in that book you gave me by the CSI lady. Buy one of those cooker lighters from the pound shop but keep it in your handbag," said Glenda.

"We still have the ecstasy tabs, however, we cannot use them as she would be up dancing all night. We do have heroin and methadone which comes in liquid form. I could pop it into her drink. I'm spoilt for choice," she mused.

"It's up to you," answered Ursula.

"She is such an obnoxious know-all, sitting in her 'baby' as she calls it. For all the world thinking she's Megan Fox in that film, *Transformers*. Bloody poser," sneered Maddie.

"What kind of film is that?" asked Glenda.

"It's a sci-fi film based on a kids' toy. Sometimes I think that woman has the IQ of a tomato plant. You know, Glenda, those toys that start as a car then turn into a robot."

"Oh yes, I remember now, Ryan had one. What a big kid she is," retorted Glenda.

"I think you are more or less there, Maddie. We could tighten things up a bit. The timing will need to be spot on. You and I will do a practice run one afternoon this week as D-Day is a week on Saturday," said Ursula.

"This flat is beginning to resemble a war cabinet," said Maddie.

"It's been a long week, girls," said Ursula. Turning to Glenda, she asked, "Are you up to date with your plans?"

"Yes, more or less, though I changed Mum and Kim's leaving to the Thursday. Moira and I leave on Friday. We couldn't stand the stress of getting our explorers away on the same day as us," shaking her head as she smiled. "They are booked into a bed and breakfast in Millport. They can't wait to go," she added.

"You have a reservation in a half decent place in Paris. The hotels there are a bit of a mixed bag. One time, I took my cousin's girl. The room was like a prison cell and the lift was a tight fit for two. We did not realise we were in the red-light district and we had to dodge the men as we left. It did not help our cause that Lauren, at sixteen, had long blonde hair, green eyes and legs up to her waist. A real stunner. It was great fun though."

"I think Moira and I are quite safe. Sounds good so far, Ursula."

"Well, goodnight ladies. As usual, plenty to think about. Remember, try and get a good night's rest. Good night again," she repeated as she got up to close the door behind them.

Chapter 68

By Tuesday, Glenda and Maddie had finished tailing Shepherd. The practice run had gone quite well. Ursula had bought a stopwatch.

As she timed Maddie, she said, "I have allowed you one hour for your sing-song. I will be waiting in Simon's car for maybe thirty minutes of that hour. When you give her whatever in your gins, I've allowed another hour for her to go quiet. The door will be opened at that point. When you slip out, light that BBQ thing."

"Right, Ursula, I will need to close the door very softly. By the way, I oiled them last time to make life easier."

"Good thinking, Maddie," she answered.

"How long will we wait in Simon's car before we leave?" asked Maddie.

"Not too sure. I reckon thirty to forty minutes at least," she replied. "That takes us to three-and-a-half hours if all goes well."

Over coffee later that day they were all strangely quiet. A cloud of depression hung over them.

"Come on, ladies," broke in Ursula. "We are nearly there. You will return from Paris next Tuesday, Glenda. Then I would like you both to concentrate on that bloody lawyer."

They both looked up, apprehension in their eyes.

"Now, that will give you something to think about," she added.

"About this lawyer, anybody any good ideas?" asked Maddie. "We should put him on the back burner for now as we have enough to think about this week? What's his name anyway?"

"Campbell McIntosh," blurted out Ursula. "I, for one, will never forget it. I will not rest till he is dealt with."

"Right, I hope you have a good time in Paris, Glenda. It is the city of love so would you try and behave yourself?" teased Maddie, trying to lift the atmosphere a little.

"Thanks for that, Maddie," added Ursula. "Now, home, ladies for an evening of rest and relaxation. I expect your house resembles a madhouse, Glenda."

"Well, somewhat," she smiled.

Friday dawned and high excitement in Glenda's house. Her mum's and Kim's cases were still open as they checked in their last minute things. Glenda had bought them both a pair of binoculars as they seemed to enjoy the wildlife.

At last, all was ready, cases closed and Mum wearing her new trendy trousers. When Moira arrived, she did a double take.

"Very nice, Mum, you really suit your new outfit."

Their mum returned a shy smile as they all piled into the car. In town, they climbed aboard McGill's bus to take them to Largs. A ten minute ferry ride to Cumbrae would follow then on to Millport at the southern end of the tiny island.

"Mum, are you sure you will be all right going on your own?" said Moira a little anxiously.

"Of course. Kim and I are used to the ferry and we like it, don't we, sweetie?" she said to Kim.

As they waved them off, Glenda said, "Now, remember and phone later to let us know you are safe. Have a lovely time, girls."

"I never thought I'd live to see the day Mum going island hopping, indeed," said Moira. "What Father would say to the breeks, I don't know," she grinned.

They both laughed as they made their way home to finish their own packing, ready for the morning.

"We are going on our own adventure," said Moira. "I can't thank you enough for this treat."

Next morning, they were off. It was Glenda's first time on a plane. Moira told her they would be travelling at four hundred miles an hour. Glenda gasped. Driving at sixty seemed too fast to her but never mind, this was a big treat, as Moira said.

Chapter 69

Arriving at their bed and breakfast hotel in Millport, Mrs Marly had the cases unpacked. Soon they were on the way to the cycle shop. The lady made a bit of a fuss over Kim, advising her of the best size. Kim chose a bright pink one with a bell and pink pompoms at the front.

"I do hope you are pleased with your choice. It's yours for the length of your stay. Are you happy with it?"

"Oh yes, and thank you," said Kim as her gran paid the cashier.

"Now, off for fish and chips at the shop," Mrs Green recommended.

The lunch was great. Kim played along the front on her bike while her gran sat on a bench happily reading her *People's Friend* magazine.

They spent four wonderful days on the island sightseeing, walking and collecting leaves and feathers for her nature notebook.

"I'm so glad your mum bought these binoculars. It's great watching the seals playing and the boats sailing past."

Two days they spent on the beach, collecting shells. They even found a large dinosaur with a red and white head, taking lots of photos. In the evening they went to the children's club.

"Gran, there are lots of games and jigsaws in here," said Kim, happy to have friends.

Her gran sat with the other mums and grans, exchanging stories and promising to return.

They both had a wonderful time. On the ferry back, with the wind blowing in their hair, Kim's granny told her, "I think some of those seals might be kelpies." Kim's eyes lit up with pleasure.

"You're joking, Gran."

"It's true," repeated her gran, "as true as my granny was a cowboy."

"You're joking, Gran, your granny was a maid. You're so funny. Now, we have to plan for Oban," said Kim as they rolled into Largs and home.

Chapter 70

Friday found Maddie a nervous wreck all day. She was quite relieved when it was time to go and meet Shepherd. The practice run yesterday went more or less to plan. It took a little longer than they thought but was not a serious problem.

Confiding in Ursula about her fears, "I'm a lot more jittery this time," she explained. "So much more than the last two. Maybe then it was all so new to us. Whereas this time, everything is planned down to the last detail and timing. Do you think I'm just scared?"

Trying to soothe Maddie's fears while putting her hand on her arm, Ursula told her, "Not a great deal we can do at this stage. For instance, if you try concentrating on keeping close to the plan, not worrying too much on what can go wrong, that may help. I admit to having a bad case of the jitters myself. That lawyer and all his badness can't stop the black hatred in me. Nights are hell."

"There is not a lot we can take for it is there? I don't think paracetamol will help."

The practice was over. Now the meeting with Allison Shepherd for the run up to the real thing tomorrow. Right, she thought, onwards and upwards. She glanced in the mirror before leaving the house. Maybe a wee dab of rouge would make me look a wee bit healthier.

Arriving slightly earlier than Shepherd she sat in the car doing her slow breathing exercises. It did help. She left the car when she heard the other lockup doors open.

Casually strolling past as Shepherd was sitting playing once more with buttons.

"Hi Beth," she called out, "that you finished work?"

"Yes," said 'Beth', "that shop gets busier by the day and my feet are killing me," she complained.

"Come and have a seat. Put your feet up and rest for a minute. I'm going out on Sunday with two friends and want to be button ready. Don't want to look like a learner, do I?"

"Oh no," said Maddie, inwardly thinking, the amount you've practiced, you should be able to drive a bloody truck.

Taking two cups and two small bottles of gin with mixers from her bag, saying, as she spied the BBQ set still on the floor, "Have a drink, Allison, I need a laugh to cheer me up tonight. Turn up the music and we'll have a sing-song."

"Thanks," replied Shepherd, "I was thinking you might want to join us on Saturday. We're going to Mingles, it's nice."

"I would love to, Allison. I'm meeting my cousin, Ruth, for dinner this week. What about next Saturday? Also, I'm going to my aunt's in Newcastle for some shopping. I'll be back Friday," she lied.

"Great. Why don't we meet here about ten-thirty on Saturday? We are never late as they have an early morning session at the gym on Sunday. They are into yoga these days," she laughed.

"I go to my aunt's by car as she doesn't drive and I like to take her out and about a bit."

"That's nice of you, Beth. I'm off now. See you tomorrow, okay!"

At that, it was a cheerio and a wave.

Chapter 71

Meeting Ursula next evening in the flat, Maddie was ready for the strong coffee which she handed her.

"Sit down, Maddie, drink that and try to settle down. Did you manage any sleep last night?" she queried.

"Not really, Ursula, the night seemed endless. Would you believe I slept in?" she went on.

"Now, put all nerves and doubts behind us, dear. She will arrive between ten-thirty and eleven. Simon's car is already in lockup two. I put it there today. We will both leave here in my car to the parking spot in the next street, leaving yours here, which is a better idea as we will both stay here tonight. You will drive Simon's car back here and I will drive mine. That means, no going back in the morning for yours." Pausing to rethink.

"Does that sound better to you? I got the bus back today. I quite enjoyed it and it passed an hour for me. Do you want me to make something to eat?"

"No thanks, Ursula, my heart is in my mouth. To be honest, I feel a little sick."

"You will have a little hot soup before we leave, just to make you feel better. This time tomorrow, it will be all over," insisted Ursula.

Ten was upon them before they knew.

"Ursula, my nerves were shattered but I was glad I went last night. I told her I was away to my aunt's in Newcastle so no one will be looking for me. I'm becoming quite an accomplished liar you know. I felt as if I had laid the groundwork so to speak."

"Good girl, Maddie. Do you have a duster and latex gloves with you?"

"Yes, I have everything I need. Also, leather."

"I'll drop you here in the next street then park next along. Now, chin up and good luck. I'll only be around the corner if you need me," she said.

Maddie had had a good stiff word with herself on the way to Lenzie. No good getting yourself in a tangle over these people. This is not just about you. It's for Ursula, Glenda, Simon, Sophie and Ryan, who did no wrong. Those people gave no thought for our children. So why should you feel guilty for repaying them?

Climbing into the car beside Allison Shepherd, her doubts evaporated.

"Hi Allison," she said.

"Hi Beth. Did you have a nice dinner?"

"Yes," replied Maddie. "Did you enjoy your night at the club?"

"Yes. I always enjoy a night out at Mingles," she answered.

Maddie produced two cups and a bottle of gin plus tonic water as Allison seemed to enjoy that mixture best. Of course, Maddie had the tonic water and tonic water as she had to stay sober. Too much to think about for gin tonight.

"Now, Allison, you can have another practice at top and windows. You must be almost perfect by now. For the life of me, I can never remember what's what. Can you press them together or must you do it one at a time?" she asked in her most annoying, naive manner.

"I'll show you again, Beth," said Allison with a touch of impatience, "I think you should stick to your own car as this one might be a bit much for you."

"Well, I do know the little arrows are for the roof to go up and down," she said, putting her finger forward as if to push the buttons.

"Don't touch the buttons," Allison almost shouted.

'Beth' jumped back. "Tell you what, why don't you turn the music up so we can have a really good sing-song?"

"Yes, great idea."

Maddie surmised she'd had maybe three or four gins in the club. In addition, she had been putting doubles in the plastic cups. The last one had a wee something extra to help her to sleep. Making it more like seven or eight. That was enough to knock out a bloody horse, thought Maddie, sitting another thirty minutes, turning down the volume of the music a little at a time.

She took the next thirty minutes to wipe everything she had touched while she counted the time, pouring the gin into the bottle so nothing was left. They would think she had drunk it at Mingles.

Maddie could hear Allison's breathing becoming shallower. I'll take a chance and take her pulse. Shit, it was almost non-existent.

Putting on her gloves, she checked she had wiped everything she could, making sure not to leave anything Shepherd had touched. I think they would know if everything was too clean. Thinking to herself, I have a feeling she has already passed. Maybe I put too much of that stuff in her drink.

At that, a quiet rapping broke the silence. Very slowly and softly, she opened the door and stepped outside.

"Ursula," she whispered. "I think she has passed already." Maddie was shaking while her voice trembled.

"Maddie, now think. Are you sure?"

"Almost certain, yes."

"Have you cleared everything up?"

"Yes, only my bag inside this door," she replied. "I never lit the BBQ."

"Just leave it. You obviously don't need it. Stand there, I'll get your bag and close the door. You go along to lockup two."

They went to Simon's car and headed home. Ursula was concerned about Maddie who, most likely, had had a bad fright.

Back at the flat, Ursula said, "Maddie, quick, get into your nightie, drink this small brandy. It will help you to sleep. We will go over and discuss it all in the morning." Ursula sat holding her hand till at last she fell over.

"It went, but not well, she might have a bad couple of days. I'll keep her here," Ursula mused.

Chapter 72

They were awake very early the next day. Sipping strong, hot coffee, both apparently lost in thought.

Breaking the silence while picking at the ribbons on her nightie, Maddie spoke.

"I'm so sorry, Ursula, scaring the living daylights out of you last night. I thought I might die of shock when I realised she had passed so soon." She dabbed her eyes as a few hot tears trickled down her cheeks. "It was totally unexpected. There was no pulse. I had surmised she would last at least to the early hours or more," she murmured. Her eyes wandered aimlessly around the room as if looking for an answer.

"I see dead people all the time, yet to sit next to her, so close, as she turned cold and white, was horrifying. I was almost sick with fear. No way could any trace of vomit be left in the car. That's what made me pull myself together, Ursula. We can't leave any evidence, we are conscious of not just one of us being caught but all three," she sobbed. "Do you think I gave her too much? Maybe it was the reaction of the booze as well. We are constantly being warned of effects of alcohol with drugs. My God, Ursula, could she put the booze back, almost like a man." She paused to think back, her eyes moving rapidly from side-to-side.

"When you know you have been the cause of it, it's enough to blow your mind. My mind is going round and round in circles trying to find a solution," she added.

"Maddie, stop," implored Ursula. "Say no more. The solution is that we don't know. Stop tying yourself in knots," she pleaded, taking Maddie's hands in hers. They were very cold, not a good sign.

"I'll make another hot drink for us while you do the toast. The police will resolve that question, not us. Our part is over," she finished.

"I'm sorry. I lost the plot for a while. Back in control now," Maddie said, gazing from the bedroom window as she gathered herself together.

"I'm not sure it's a good idea to mention this to Glenda. She would only get herself in a tangle."

"I hope she is enjoying Paris. The wee soul has never been further than Ayr and that for the Sunday School trip," Maddie added.

"I expect it will be somewhat of a culture shock, all that colour and style. A wee bit different from Sauchiehall Street. She will love it. Even the warmer weather will cheer her up," agreed Ursula.

"Paris! I'm really here, Moira. I can't believe it, me in Paris. It's like another world," said Glenda, gazing around her in wonder. Their hotel was central. They unpacked quickly then had coffee in the hotel lounge. Next, a stroll along the River Seine to Notre Dame.

"I have made a list of places to see. Most of all I would like to see Monet's house and garden in Giverny. We will have to make a day of it. Remember to wear your handbag around your neck as Paris is famous for pickpockets. We will be on the train and metro so be very careful. Now, back for dinner and you choose where you would like to visit."

Next day, they arrived at Monet's house and garden.

"I've never seen such a wonderful place in my life. We must have our photo taken on the bridge. Row upon row of flowers, roses, clematis and the water garden. Superb," said Moira.

Lunch next and then the house with yellow and blue everywhere.

As they walked through the iris garden, Moira said to Glenda, her eyes sparkling, "You know that song, Glenda, *This is my lovely day*, well this is mine."

Next day, they took a trip on the Bateaux cruise boat along the Seine. Glenda bought a charcoal drawing from an artist, signed and dated.

"I have a real piece of art. I widna ca' the Queen my cousin, as they say," she smiled.

They had a morning in a wonderful shop, Galeries Lafayette.

"I thought it was a museum, not a shop," gasped Glenda.

The next day was a rush to see all they could. Moira loved the chic French ladies, 'less is more', fashion-wise. Glenda was fascinated by the variety of men's moustaches, people eating outside and the smell of Nutella crepes everywhere they went. She bought her mum a real silk scarf and a few packets of lavender soaps and bags. All too soon, it was over.

On the plane home, Moira read her book she'd bought at Monet's house.

"Glenda, whenever I smell a rose, I will be back in that garden. Thank you. Did you remember to put Mum's scarf in the Galeries Lafayette bag?"

"Yes. She will love it. A real silk scarf from Paris. Wow," said Moira in the plane, tired out.

Chapter 73

Deep in thought, Ursula was at home contemplating what they'd done, the enormity of it. Bottom line, it was murder, punishable by life imprisonment. Dismissing her fear, instead concentrating her mind on any mistakes they may have made.

I should be focussing on the next assignment, not bloody worrying about things I can't change and are over. Her mind repeatedly drifted back to that lawyer, Campbell McIntosh. A devious parasite, despicable in every way. In truth, he was more to blame than Matt Thomson. He used and abused the law, getting guilty people off for profit.

Glancing at Simon's photo brought to her mind that even worse day than the court case where they all sat there like so many assorted fat toads, not even an apology for his family, nothing.

As the doorbell rang, she answered it to James.

"Come in, James, have a seat while I make us some coffee," she said, glad of the distraction. As she brought in the drinks, James explained.

"Thanks for that, Ursula. I hope you are feeling a little more settled. Are your classes helping?" he asked. "I'm here about the headstone for Simon. This is the brochure," he added as he handed a glossy catalogue to her. "You choose which one you like and what you would like written on it."

"How kind," she replied. "I'll get back to you. I think I would like a couple of lines from John Donne's poem." She smiled as they sipped their drinks.

"Have you lost weight, James? Are you well?" Thinking to herself he looked terrible. She had never seen him look so haggard and old.

"I'm fine. It's been a distressing time for us all," he paused, obviously not knowing what to say. "When the police came that day, I thought it was a mistake of some kind.

However, they had those pictures," he murmured. "That's what made it so hard, Ursula. For him to be killed like that, doing no wrong, while that horrid man roared off, leaving my boy dead in the road. People who seen him were shocked beyond belief. Women holding their children close, hiding their eyes." Ursula could see he was reliving the scene.

"When they came here," said Ursula, "much to my shame, I never asked any questions, standing there dumbstruck, my brain was frozen. It was like a dream, it could not be true, they must be lying or have the wrong person," she babbled out.

"One man took his number and phoned the police," James said but couldn't go on. He lowered his head into his hands, almost afraid to look at her.

She gazed at him, so like her Simon. She could not find any words to help. Anger rose in her throat, almost choking her, her grief as fresh as on the day the police broke the dreadful news. She couldn't hold back a gasping sob.

Raising his head and taking a deep breath, James took control. "Ursula, drink your coffee and be at peace with yourself," he said kindly, his eyes moist. "I will have to go back to the office. Are you sure you will be okay?"

"Yes, yes, I'll be fine, don't worry about me, James. Thank you, I'll see you to the door." As it closed, she sat down, feeling more determined than ever, telling herself vehemently, "No, no, Mr Campbell McIntosh, no more Mrs Nice Guy, I'm not done with you. Not by a long chalk. James's visit was just the spur I needed. You will most certainly be paid in full. Just you wait and see."

Chapter 74

Maddie had spent the weekend in a lather of worry and a horrible feeling of dread. She could hardly content herself to sit down. Bloody stop it, she told herself. Her legs were shaking and her insides were not full of butterflies but crows.

She was glad to be on her way to the flat to meet Ursula. Glenda would be back too. The thought made her feel a bit better. Get a grip, Maddie, she scolded herself.

As they both waited for Glenda, Ursula said, "Now, Maddie, I hope you are a little better. It was a tough one, however, it's history. So, a smile on for Glenda. You know she can smell fear a mile away. She is one clever girl for seeing if you are upset, so chin up."

At that, Glenda arrived.

"I'm so glad to see you two," as she hugged Maddie and then Ursula. "Tell me, how was it? I'll bet it was not pleasant, Maddie, because, unlike the others, you were up close to her."

"How was your trip, Glenda?" asked Ursula.

"It was wonderful but tell me all about Saturday. Has there been any news about her in the papers?"

"Nothing as yet, Glenda. I suspect her parents would pay to have it kept out. Or even put it down to an accidental death," added Ursula.

"But they might not be able to keep it out of the *Herald* or the *Times*," explained Maddie. "People will want to know the where and when of the funeral," she continued. "What do you think, Ursula?"

"I expect you might be right. On the other hand, we will just have to be patient and wait," she responded.

"Sometimes, these accidents are put down to sudden death syndrome," suggested Glenda. "Tell me what happened on Saturday. Did you have to use the BBQ set or were the other things enough?"

"There was enough, Glenda, but we think she had a lot more to drink at the club than we first thought," she added.

"You are right, Maddie, you can never tell with drink. Were you okay on the night or scared skinny?" she went on.

Hell, there was no kidding Glenda. She's a mum in every way, thought Maddie, at the same time replying, "I was fine, Glenda. Stressed out but we managed okay," she lied, giving Ursula a swift guilty glance.

Ursula made tea and a snack. As she served it, she thought to herself, well, here goes.

"As you know, ladies, I can't get that lawyer off my mind. He will not get away with it if I have anything to do with it, he will not. Furthermore, did any of these parents bother to send a sympathy card. No, not a bloody word. Their silence speaks volumes. I hate them, that's why I'm able to do this. My hatred keeps me going." She almost spat the words out. "Even that parasite of a lawyer, not a bloody syllable of sympathy. I'll get that bastard if it's the last thing I do," she stormed.

"Please don't go upsetting yourself anymore, Ursula. It's so unlike you," said Glenda, handing her a cup of tea.

"If you don't want to help in this one, I will understand, however, I will need help in tailing him."

"Ursula, we started together and we will complete this the same way," replied Maddie.

"Agreed," said Glenda. "After all the help you have given us, we will be with you."

"I'm thinking some kind of road traffic accident as that is what he specialises in."

"How tragic," answered Maddie.

"And so young," added Glenda.

"My plan is for us to have a week off, catching up with our lives. My daughter for one is beginning to worry about me so forget about everything but resting. Maybe there will be some news about the Shepherd woman by then. I'm so sorry for losing my temper ladies, it's not good to bottle things up. Who can I tell but you two?" she added.

"I will make fresh coffee and you, Ursula, settle down and forget everything. Because Glenda is going to entertain us with her account of Paris."

They spent a lovely hour reliving Glenda's trip.

"By the way, girls, I brought you two back some wonderful lavender soap," said Glenda.

"Well, that's it. Remember this is a week of catching up. If I get any news, I will phone. Don't worry," said Ursula, a little calmer now. At that, they all left, one by one, as usual.

Chapter 75

DS McNeil was holding a stack of folders as he entered DI Diamond's office.

"Good morning, Sir, a lot to go through today," he said as he put the pile on Diamond's desk.

"Morning, Andrew. Let's get started then. I have to admit, the newspapers have been more than helpful. Keeping the whole situation in the public eye. I'm amazed at the reaction of parents who have been extremely good at coming forward with names and places. Some, at no small risk to themselves. Lots of tiddlers have been caught and are off the streets. Quite a few have court dates already."

"That's great, Sir, just goes to show what a concentrated effort can do. We have managed to, near enough, halve the amount of dealers on the streets in all three cities," continued DS McNeil.

"I'm well pleased," Diamond went on. "So, let's see what we have here."

As McNeil opened the top folder, scanning it, Diamond commented, "Not so many fatalities these last two months. I see two in Dundee and one in Glasgow, however, three in Edinburgh. All of the deaths were the usual overdoses of drugs. The bad batch appears to have stopped. Yet, in my experience, they put it away and then bring it back. We will need to watch very carefully for that bad batch reappearing.

"I also hear from Dundee's team, they are quite near getting one of the big boys. Seemingly, he stayed a week over his time. It will not be us but it might be the money men who charge him. As you know, all the banks have a fraud department these days, but, as ever, it's wait and see," Diamond said.

"These folders are all just for you to sign. Just two for you to go over. One is a young doctor from Lenzie. She seemingly had taken a small dose of something. However, her blood alcohol reading was 140 milligrams. The doctor said she could have died with that amount plus the heroin. What do you want to do? Will we visit her family or what? She has her own flat in Lenzie. Also, she was found Sunday, about six in the evening, by two flatmates, in her own car at her nearby lockup," said McNeil.

"Not a whole lot we can do if people wish to drink themselves to death. We will go tomorrow and visit her folks. You get the address. Sometimes, in these cases, parents just want to forget about it and grieve in peace. What do you make of it, Andrew?"

"I feel so sorry for parents who lose their children. They have done the best they can. She was well under ten stone, a hell of a lot of booze even for a big man. It's so sad," he commiserated.

"One more to go. A young man found by the local coppers. He was out of his mind with too much booze so he had a night in the cells then let out in the morning. His dad asked if you could give him a warning as he is only sixteen. His exact words were could you give him a bit of a fright. I said you would. Might keep him out of any more trouble in future," said McNeil.

"What do they want me to do? Skelp his backside? That's what they should have done only more often," laughed Diamond. "Well, all in all, Andrew, our drugs scene is more or less under control. We are making headway and that's the best we can do," finished Diamond as DS McNeil left with his signed folders.

Chapter 76

Ursula met her daughter, Ruth, for lunch and some shopping. It was so nice to spend time together for a change.

"This is like old times, Mum," said Ruth. "I'll find out if there is anything good on at the Edinburgh Playhouse. Then go to the *Cosmos* for dinner. I love it there but we must be on time as there is always a large queue.

"I will love that. Also, on the train, so no parking worries."

Saturday, they took themselves off to the Livingstone outlet. Ursula felt as if she had rejoined the ranks of the human race. They treated themselves to new handbags and shoes, which they did not need but, hey ho.

In the evening, she caught up with her cross-stitch, long neglected, and two books to quietly read.

Next day, visiting friends who now had new grandchildren. Little treats but treats nonetheless.

Moira had the decorator in so she and Glenda went round to their older sister, Jane.

"It's so nice to see you girls," she smiled. She was very much like their mum, gentle and kind. "First, the kettle on and I have a fresh apple pie. I expect you two are off shopping if I know anything."

"We are going for curtains, cushion covers and cups and saucers in her new colours of grey, pink and purple, Jane, which I suspect is the same colour scheme as Monet's garden," teased Glenda. "However, Jane," she said, becoming more serious, "I would like your advice about a wee problem I've been thinking over for a while.

"Mum is paying rent in her wee flat while I have a spare room. It's time I opened Ryan's room, redecorated it and maybe Mum would like to move in with Kim and I," she queried.

"I think that's a wonderful idea, Glenda," answered Jane. "Mum would be so happy with the company. When I went round to visit, Mum and Kim were at the table editing her photo albums and notebooks from the trips to Millport and Dunoon. They informed me their next adventure is Oban. I must admit it was a surprise to see Mum in her new trousers. She looked so happy. She has a lovely new bedroom suite and bed so nothing needs to be bought. As you know, we will all help with the room, Glenda, you cannot keep it as a shrine forever."

"I agree," said Moira. "You ask her tonight. She will be as pleased as punch."

"That's settled, Jane, so we are off to the shops. And I fancy fish and chips for tea tonight, ladies," answered Glenda, so happy to have her sister's advice. She had been worrying about it for a while.

Maddie had made good use of her week which she spent with her mother who had decided they would have the living room redecorated in nice bright colours. Maddie took her shopping in town. She bought two large vases, filling them with the irises she had seen in Maddie's book. Pink, yellow and mauve. I love those flowers," Mrs Price said.

"Mum they are large enough for a hotel foyer," protested Maddie.

"I like them," she insisted. "I'm fed up with being a mousey old woman. In your pictures, the ladies, even old ladies are smart and chic."

Chic, thought Maddie, what next?

"Maybe next time, you could take me," she added.

"I will that's a promise, Mum, next year, I will, so start saving," thinking, I hope we never go to Africa. It would be lions, elephants and multi-coloured turbans. She smiled to herself. "Maybe you might like Paris instead of Rome. It's all colour in Paris and the shops are out of this world," she told her and thought, I can't wait to get back to the flat and two sane ladies. I must admit, this week has cheered me up wonderfully.

Chapter 77

They were fully aware of this last enterprise, besides which, just how important it was to Ursula. Sunday saw them in the flat. Ursula, as usual, had coffee ready.

Trying to be cheerful, Glenda said, "I had a nice time with Mum and Kim lunching out and shopping. Also, I met up with all my sisters in Jane's house."

Maddie noticed she had been biting her nails again.

"They said I was looking less stressed. Moira said it was the classes. Sarah asked if I was finding them helpful. Definitely, I told her, most supportive."

Maddie teased her saying, "You are a natural born liar, Glenda."

"And getting better at it every day," said Glenda.

"I hope *you* had a restful week, Maddie?" inquired Ursula.

"Restful? Not a chance with my mother and her redecorating. She has taken to lunching out which entails shopping in the mornings, lunch and more shopping before trudging home. I must admit, I'm glad of her. She is quite good fun. Her flower arrangements are big enough for the Central Hotel's foyer though!" said Maddie, shaking her head.

"What about you, Ursula? Did you have a relaxing time? I hope you didn't mope about, thinking and planning."

"No, Maddie, I put everything on the back burner. Ruth took charge. She maintained I looked a bit peaky, her words not mine. We went to the Playhouse in Edinburgh. Also, a really good restaurant, *Cosmo*. Try and go there, ladies. We did some shopping and the art gallery too. As you know, I love quiet time with my cross stitch and books. To be honest, for the last year I've done little else but plot and plan," she said, rubbing her hands together as if she was cold. "Not good for me," she added.

"Now, down to business," straightening up and gathering herself together, she went on. "Ladies, there has been nothing in the newspapers about Allison Shepherd. This is beginning to worry me. I'm asking why not, myself."

"Sometimes, Ursula, the papers do not print a story if requested by the family not to," answered Maddie. "She did work in Stobhill Hospital however, she was moved. I'm not sure where. I'm back in the Royal tomorrow. There is bound to be a lot of gossip about her. I'll try and sniff around."

"I'm back in Stobhill tomorrow as well, Ursula. I'm in the clinic with a client. I do sometimes meet nurses and carers who go for tea. There may be something said. The drawback is they might not say to me because they know about Ryan."

"Again, it is wait and see. I'll get tomorrow's *Herald* and *Times* and look in the hatch, match and dispatch columns. They may have something.

"Now, about this bloody lawyer. Any great ideas, ladies?" she asked.

"I suggest a road traffic accident as there is no way we can get near enough to give him any drugs," said Maddie.

"The best way to deal with him is to put up a board for the next few weeks. Tailing him will have to be done by us all," said Ursula.

"Also, Ursula, we need to be ultra cautious with this man. He will have all sorts of contacts. He gets even an inkling of anyone tailing him, there will be a private detective on our tails to have a look see," warned Maddie. "At the same time," she continued, "he knows all kinds of criminals. I imagine him able to get in touch with quite unsavoury people. People like himself, nasty, vicious and will do almost anything for money," Maddie finished.

"I think you read him right, Maddie. I watched him in court. Thomson, Simon's killer, never spoke a word that day. McIntosh more or less ignored him. When the charge was read out, the lawyer rose and addressed the judge. He stated there was no charge to answer because the police had made a mistake over the readings. That was that. Thomson was dismissed. He had paid ten thousand pounds for this to McIntosh.

"Thomson went over, most likely to thank him, holding out his hand. It was James who pointed that out. McIntosh gathered his papers, turned his back on him and hurried away. Never even gave him the time of day.

"The whole place was stunned into silence. The police were as astonished as everyone else. Nasty man. I would not like to ever be in his bad books, I'll tell you that."

This was the first time that Glenda and Maddie had heard Ursula's story. Now they understood the deep hatred that Ursula could not get over.

"That is reason enough for us to be extra cautious even if it takes us longer," said Maddie.

"So is that the plan for this week? We all take a turn at watching him working in his office. Also, in court. Take special note of times for the board. Maddie, you do his office in the mornings as you are late this week. I will do afternoons. Also, I'll have a peek at that road if I have a chance," explained Ursula. "Glenda, will you tail the wife if you can? Better to keep an eye on her as well. Never know what will turn up. We can change times and places as needs must.

"We may need some different colours of wigs and some outfits to blend in, in court, or maybe pretend to work in a nearby office," she continued.

"We meet here on Saturday this week as there might be some news about Shepherd. They cannot put a funeral off for too much longer."

Chapter 78

Finishing work early had enabled Glenda to have a recce around Dullatur, first the old village then move on to the big houses. She had noticed there were only two entrances, one coming down from Cumbernauld or the motorway, the other from Kilsyth. Handy, she thought, dressed today, in her taxi driver's gear and driving Simon's car with the taxi sign on the front. A stranger here would quickly attract attention and maybe questions. She had passed two dogwalkers who gave her a look, driving around as if looking for a particular address. At the road end, she parked, sitting as if checking her phone, watching the raindrops dancing down the windowpane. This is scary, she mused. Stop it, dismiss that notion right now, she scolded herself.

When suddenly, Mrs McIntosh came out of the front door, into her car and whizzed off in a hurry.

Glenda followed, where she entered the roundabout, then the Glasgow turnoff, staying in the middle lane, then coming off at Great Western Road. Keeping two cars behind, Glenda kept up. Quite a way along, she turned into a drive. Glenda stopped across the road turning into a side street. She could see the door from here. A much younger, handsome guy came out.

"Hallo darling." At the same time, holding her close, kissing her passionately as they entered the house, arms entwined around each other.

"My, my," Glenda exclaimed. "That was a bolt from the blue."

Taking off, then turning into the first side street and parking. Changing her auburn wig for a black one, also her grey jacket for a red. She could see Mrs McIntosh's car from her vantage point. While waiting, she took her notebook out to catch up. The lady was in lover boy's home for one hour and thirty minutes. As she left, her hair was tied up in a ponytail. The same hugs and kisses were repeated on the doorstep.

Glenda thought cheekily, I wonder if there's a queue for that. She moved back into the main road. The traffic was building up now. Tailing her back onto the motorway where she stopped at Sainsbury's. She shopped for another thirty minutes and then headed home.

Keeping up, Glenda thought the antics of the working classes never fails to amaze. Her brow wrinkling up in puzzlement. I wonder what Ursula will make of this little tail, she thought as she headed home.

After school, Ursula spent the rest of the day driving up and down the Coach Road, the road from the main Glasgow to Falkirk road up to Dullatur. The bottom end had a couple of farms, one of which had a riding school which made for a bit of horse traffic, lots of young people moving from field to field. One would need to be careful as the road was extremely narrow in places and treacherous for drivers as there were lots of sharp bends further up. Not a great deal of traffic. Ursula imagined it would be a nightmare in wet conditions especially in the dark. There were two trees, more or less growing over the road which would reduce the passing room.

Perfect for our purposes I expect, she told herself. Also, she noticed high verges on either side with tall trees reducing the light even more. More than likely, this was an old drovers' road, long before coaches. Not a lot I can do here. I'll report back to Maddie and Glenda. It will be useful to know what they think.

Maddie looked and felt quite elegant in her black suit and blonde bobbed wig. She was supposed to be a legal secretary in Glasgow not too far away from Campbell McIntosh's office in Merchant City. This being her day off, she had watched him entering his office at nine this morning. He left with two colleagues, one male, one female, for lunch in a nearby restaurant at twelve-thirty. She had finished her packed lunch where she sat in an old graveyard watching the small birds when he appeared to be leaving his office about two-thirty. Where the hell is he going, she asked herself. She followed him to his parking place. Thank goodness I'm parked nearby.

Leading her over the River Clyde to the south side of the city, he parked in a lovely cul-de-sac. These were very upmarket tenements having four or five bedrooms which nowadays went for a great deal of money. The main door, which was opened by a very trendy, upmarket blonde, faced towards the street.

"Come in sweetie," trilled the blonde.

Sweetie, thought Maddie. That's rich. Bet you a fiver she doesn't come cheap. There were lots of parking spaces as most people would be at work. He was in her house for one hour and forty minutes. Then he returned to his office where he stayed till six, then headed for home, where most likely, wee wifey would await him all showered and dressed ready for dinner.

Maddie made for home. It had been a long day. More importantly, a great deal of information for Ursula.

Chapter 79

After lunch, the ladies looked out their notebooks.

"You go first, Glenda," said Ursula.

"I had a good look round Dullatur. It's a beautiful place with top of the range houses. However, it would be easy to be spotted. I, of course, being a taxi-driver looking for an address, was ignored. I waited outside her house, well up the street a bit. She came out in a hurry, about two-thirty. Following her onto the motorway, where she made for Glasgow, Great Western Road to be precise, where she met her lover in his house. I could hardly believe it." Pausing to think and reread her notes. "She was in there for one-and-a-half hours. I would believe it of him but you could have knocked me down with a feather. Kissing and cuddling on the bloody doorstep if you please," burst out Glenda.

Maddie and Ursula were laughing at Glenda's face.

"Buggers," said Maddie.

Ursula made another coffee. Handing one to Glenda, she teased, "For the shock, Glenda." They all giggled.

"Do you have anything for us, Maddie?" Ursula asked.

"Before I tell you, I heard a rumour in the hospital, about Allison Shepherd but no one can say if it's true. Seemingly, they said she had died. On the other hand, no one knows the cause. But no more information was forthcoming.

"So it's wait and see again," said Ursula. "I think the funeral notice will be in the paper this week." Shrugging her shoulders as if to mean 'no news yet'.

"Right, Maddie, what have you got for us?"

"I was dressed as a secretary and waited in the car park around the block. He and two colleagues went for lunch. Returned to his office. Then about two-thirty he left again, into his car and drove over to the south side. He parked in a very upmarket cul-de-sac. Large tenements with a price tag to match. A very trendy blonde opened the door. *'Come in sweetie,'* she uttered. By the looks of her she is no lovelorn girlfriend. She is most certainly a high-class hooker or I'm a monkey's uncle. A specialist of some kind," stressed Maddie.

Ursula and Glenda stared at Maddie.

"Heavens," stuttered Ursula, "it gets better."

"He was in there an hour and forty minutes. Bet that cost him," Maddie went on.

"Now, my turn, ladies. That road is a nightmare. Very narrow in places. There are two farms at the bottom. One is a riding school with mums, dads and kids arriving and leaving all the time. On the other hand, that is in the morning. We will be doing our business about seven when it is beginning to get dark. If it's raining, much better for us. High verges and tall trees will be helpful too. There are two really tricky places. Glenda, did you notice them?" she asked, turning towards Glenda.

"Well, I did, Ursula. I suggest we become ramblers on Sunday. The weather is fine. Park at the road end. Take our cameras and take our time," she concluded.

"You're brilliant, Glenda, great idea," gasped Maddie.

"You know what she's after, don't you, Maddie? She has caught the dressing up bug. This time a rambler with walking boots, anorak and the woolly scarf," teased Ursula. "Great. But seriously, this is the scariest one yet. In addition, that road is difficult. Carry on with the tailing. I'll help with the wife. It is very important we have as much information to hand as it's possible to have," she said.

Glenda nodded as she filled out the board. Maddie, looking at Ursula, felt she was very, very nervous this time. And she still had no definite on Shepherd. Which was a worry.

Chapter 80

Tuesday morning found Maddie in court, dressed this time, as a reporter. Black trench coat, auburn wig and carrying a large handbag filled with notebooks, giving the appearance of being a very busy lady.

Glancing around, what a place to find yourself in. She had only been in a courtroom once before and never wished to repeat that experience.

Watching Campbell McIntosh work, or more like, perform, was a masterclass. He was a winner, no doubt, precise and competent. You could almost smell it in his every move. Wasting no time, stating his case in clipped sentences. Not a smile, this man knows his stuff. I have a feeling, she thought, he would not take kindly to losing. That must be the reason his fees were so high.

There were two cases this morning, both drink-driving offences. Maddie watched the judge. He said very little, a nod now and then, but missed nothing. His eyes roving from lawyer to client as if searching them for the truth.

The first man, Robert Bell, received a hefty fine in addition to losing his licence for a year. Furthermore, he would have to resit his driving test. The second gentleman did not get off so lightly.

The judge told him, "This is a very serious offence, Mr McNab. I am imposing a fine of seven-hundred-and-fifty pounds. You will lose your licence for one year at the end of which you will resit your test. Besides this, you will attend rehabilitation classes for your alcohol problem."

He looked very serious. Maddie surmised, I am nervous just hearing him. Both men appeared satisfied. Maybe they'd been expecting custodial sentences.

McIntosh closed his folder. Not a word or even a glance towards his clients. He thanked the judge, turned and left.

"Obnoxious swine," Maddie whispered under her breath. "Wonder how much that display of bad manners had cost these gentlemen."

Leaving, as most people had left, she made for the flat. There, she changed her clothes and Simon's car for her own. Heading for work, normality and lunch in the canteen.

Glenda had taken over McIntosh's wife. Her first port of call was the hairdresser's then the nail bar to have long pink extensions added.

In both places she was greeted with, "Good morning, Mrs McIntosh. How are you today?"

"I'm fine, Amy," was the reply at the hairdresser's as the young lady escorted her to the sinks while the other took her coat.

She must be a regular but not much familiarity with the staff.

Twelve-thirty, she was finished with both shops. Heading for the garage near the roundabout, where she filled her car, near which was a Chinese restaurant. Not, of course, the usual takeaway, but a really nice place. Quite upmarket. Following her inside, Glenda found a seat at the back from where she could see her and hear the conversation. It was buffet service. Helping herself to a soup and a sweet, she sat down.

Mrs Mcintosh was joined by two ladies of similar age and appearance. Smiling pleasantly, they greeted her.

"Hallo Cassie, have you been to Angela's? Oh, I see you have," as she took in the pink nails. "She does a super job of nails, I must agree."

"I have an appointment tomorrow. You've also been to Amy's by the look of that hairdo," the other lady added, at the same time pulling out a chair and taking a seat.

"I really like her plus it saves me having to drive into town every week," answered Cassie.

At least we know her name now, thought Glenda.

"Are you going to Sally's birthday bash next Saturday evening?" she inquired.

"Sure am. I, for one, am looking forward to it. Are you going?" asked the blonde one.

"Yes, we are," Cassie replied, nodding.

An hour was whiled away with gossip and small talk.

"I have to get moving, girls, as Campbell is home sharp today. We are going out to dinner with two of his colleagues. Business, you know," she explained.

Glenda paid, left, and sat in the car park watching as they left together, air kissing each other, making for their own cars. Reflecting, as she started her own car, what a hard life these ladies have. No need to follow anymore today, she is heading home, as I am.

Maddie waited outside McIntosh's office on Thursday. He came out at two-thirty. Instead of going to the West End, he headed the opposite way. This road, I'm sure, takes him to Falkirk. Where the hell is he going, she pondered. So why not stay on the motorway? After a few turns, she did not know, they were on a road to Haggs. Continuing for about a mile where a large sign appeared. *Turn left for Antonine Village. Four-bedroom homes for sale.* Which he did, and she followed slowly. He then stopped in the village at a small old cottage, one among six as far as she could make out. The new builds were further up the hill. Stopping to get her bearings a little further on, looking at her notebook as if lost, she saw him at the door which was opened by a very pretty young woman.

"Hello darling," they both uttered at the same time, as he disappeared inside.

"Hell," exclaimed Maddie. "It gets bloody worse. The mind boggles at this guy."

She continued up to the new builds. Six in all, two sold and four for sale. Extremely modern and smart. She took her time writing all the details. After fifteen minutes, she left, parking on the opposite side at the shops. He was inside for one-and-a-half hours, then passed her.

Waiting ten minutes, she headed for the motorway home. He had not far to go home. Poor sod, he was bound to be tired out.

Wonder what Ursula will make of this, she queried.

Chapter 81

As they had a bit of catching up to do, the ladies were early on Sunday. Ursula, as usual, had a light lunch ready.

"Did anyone manage that back road?" inquired Ursula.

"I did, but only once in the evening," said Glenda. "It's in my diary for Wednesday. Changing the subject I tailed his wife this week, not lover boy. By the way, her name is Cassandra, Cassie to her friends." Glenda paused to read her notes. "She, like him, is a piece of work. Hairdressers twice this week. Once for a shampoo and set, next for her roots. Wednesday, beauty parlour for pink nail extensions and a pedicure. Out to lunch with two girlfriends, which took nearly two hours. I heard her say she was going out to dinner that night with hubby and two of his work colleagues. I must admit she does have a really hard life," finished Glenda.

"It sounds very difficult," interrupted Maddie. "Does that mean she only sees lover boy one day a week? Unlike her husband, who has two."

Ursula laughed. "Do tell, Maddie."

"I followed him on Thursday to a small village just past Haggs. Antonine Village, it's called. It's six or so old cottages, beautiful place. However, there are new builds further up the hill. Anybody going, you can pretend to be a potential buyer."

Glenda said, "So the dirty rotten swine has two bits on the side. One in the West End and one in the country. Ursula, we would be doing the world a favour to get rid of him." Turning to Maddie and Ursula, Glenda could understand the wife's feelings as she had been in that position.

"Hold on, Glenda, she is playing him at his own game," Maddie answered. "Bit of luck, the bugger could get a STD," she added.

Ursula interjected, "Ladies, stop. Glenda, you make the coffee. Maddie, you start filling in the board."

"I have done that road a few times this week at different times. Mornings, it is busy. Mums with prams. As you know, horses are ruled by their stomachs. They will go to anyone with a lump of sugar or an apple. The riding school seems to be busier in the afternoons." She glanced down at her notes before continuing. "We will more than likely be doing our business between six-thirty and seven-thirty. It will need to be a Tuesday or a Thursday as far as I can see but it's where?" she asked.

"As I suggested before, we should dress up as ramblers next Sunday morning. We can park our cars at the bottom of the road and walk up to the top. That will let us see up close the most dangerous places. What do you think, Ursula?" she asked.

"Brilliant, Glenda. That's the answer," added Maddie.

"Good thinking, Glenda," said Ursula, "but I know you. Anything to dress up," she teased. "The good news, Maddie, is the Shepherd woman's funeral is next Friday morning."

They could both see the relief on Maddie's face. "Thank God," was all she said.

"Then we meet at ten on Sunday. Boots and anoraks, ladies," Ursula continued.

"I will have to see if I can get anymore on all three ladies," said Maddie. "If it wasn't so serious, it would be funny," she told them. "Those two are made for one another, both double-dealing, devious bastards. Maybe it would be better if she was in the car too," she said, looking from one to the other.

"No, no," said Glenda, "we are only seeing to him. Let her do all the whoring and touring she wants, she'll soon get sick of it."

"Anyway, you're right," continued Maddie, "she'll soon see her friends melt away like snow off a dyke. They may play away from home but they like to keep a facade of respectability and it will come out. We will make sure of that. It's Glasgow, not London we're talking about," she mocked. "None of these people will want a young, good-looking widow hanging about like a loose cannonball," she went on. "They will drop her like a hot potato in less than three months. Watch and see."

"I would agree," said Ursula. "Seen it all before. Is the board finished? Well done. Maddie, you are on him this week. Glenda, you keep your eye on the wife and I'll do the road. Sunday, we're all together. This has been a good day's work."

At that, they made for home.

Chapter 82

DI Diamond had been extremely busy over the last couple of months. Trying to collate the feedback from all four cities. DS McNeil entered carrying a neat stack of folders.

"Good morning, Sir. These have just to be signed," he explained.

Breathing a sigh of relief, Diamond smiled, "Thanks Andrew. As far as I can make out, there has been a general improvement in our situation," as he put the folders to one side. "Two factors helped. The involvement of the newspapers as well as the police from all four cities working together. We also got help from Aberdeen. I will be sending letters of thanks to all concerned. What do you have, Andrew?"

DS McNeil, looking over his notebook, answered, "The big boys are conspicuous by their absence. We are seeing quite a difference in the drug scene. Street dealers have become very shy while the tiddlers are struggling to make a living. Quite a few have been charged, the rest have flown the coop. They will not have an easy time if they try to muscle in on the London or Manchester territory. It will be outright war," he finished.

"Glasgow has seen an increase in gang warfare. Clubs are complaining of not being busy," said Diamond.

McNeil replied, "What do they expect when they kill their clients with bad stock? Although, about that young doctor from Lenzie, the pathologist suggested the alcohol was more to blame than the drug. I will not mention the amount to her parents."

"We will visit them in the morning, Andrew. Make it about ten. That's it for today, thanks," Diamond finished.

They arrived at the appointed time to a large house, a long drive and a well-tended garden. Trees at the back assured them of privacy. Mr and Mrs Shepherd invited them in.

"Come in, gentlemen. Thank you for coming," Mr Shepherd said.

They were an older couple. Mrs Shepherd invited them to have a seat.

"Sit here," she said. They sat in the large comfortable living room. Mrs Shepherd was nervous like most people faced with a similar situation.

Both men could see they were at a loss to understand. The mother spoke first.

"She was our only child. We were late in having her. She never lacked for anything in her life. I admit she was a little spoiled," she sobbed. "Her father gave her the money for that car. He could deny her nothing. Her friend had one and Alison fell in love with it. She wanted it so she got it. She was our pride and joy," Mrs Shepherd whispered softly.

Her husband putting his arm around her, trying in vain to console her, continued, "Seemingly, she was alone in the car. She had said she liked to practice with the controls, putting the top back. I know she had been out for a drink with friends. That's why she was sitting and not driving."

"We are extremely sorry for your loss, Mr and Mrs Shepherd. The doctor thinks it was the mixture of alcohol in combination with something else she had taken earlier," DI Diamond told them.

They did not answer, only looked at him blankly.

Once again, both offered their condolences. The parents saw them to the door.

"I am sorry I have no further explanation but again we both offer our sympathy.

In the car, Diamond turned to Andrew.

"The sooner people understand that too much alcohol can be dangerous, the better.

"They should put a warning on the bottles, same as cigarettes," replied DS McNeil.

Chapter 83

Maddie and Glenda took turns this week in following McIntosh. On Tuesday, Maddie tailed him to the West End flat where he stayed for about an hour then he returned to his office. She wished she could be a fly on the wall. What was the sleazy bugger up to? Wonder how much it cost for her. She returned home consumed with curiosity.

On Thursday, Glenda waited outside his office. She was beginning to worry but stayed with it. However, he left at four making for the motorway as Maddie had said he would.

She had never travelled this road before. They came off at Haggs, took a left for about one-and-a-half miles. There was the large sign for the village. She had guessed it would be more difficult than it was. She knew it was just nerves. If this man spotted her, the game was up so just keep calm, go and view your house.

Watching as he stopped at a beautiful little cottage, holding a bottle. Sneaky shit, she thought trying to buy her off with a bottle of wine. Creep.

"Hello darling," he said as he held the pretty young woman close. My, thought Glenda, that creep can smile, as he entered the door, clutching the bottle.

At that, Glenda drove up to the new builds. Really nice, she mused, getting out to take a walk around. Twenty minutes later, she started back down, parking on the opposite side of the road. This was a good time to change her wig and jacket. Also, to put her taxi sign in her window.

An hour later, she observed him returning down the hill, staying on the main road. Then up the Coach Road and home. Glenda made for the motorway and home.

Early Sunday morning, Ursula went to the cemetery carrying flowers for Simon's grave. The stone, chosen by James, was black marble with gold lettering. She had chosen the wording from *The Anniversary* by John Donne, one of her favourite poets.

All other things, to their destruction draw,

Only our love hath no decay.

A silent tear slipped down her cheek as she left to meet her ladies.

Maddie and Glenda waited at the road end as Ursula arrived, dressed as she was, in their ramblers' outfits.

"Ready to go, ladies?" she asked. "It looks quite different when you're walking. It's beautiful and peaceful."

"Yes," they both agreed.

Taking their time and taking notes of all they saw. The road was narrow with barely enough room for two cars to pass. Halfway up they crossed a small bridge.

"It doesn't look too safe to me," said Glenda. "Only one car could pass here so people would have to honk their horns as they approached."

"That might be fine on a bright day but nor such a clever move in the dark or if it was wet and slippery from heavy rain," continued Maddie.

"Will I mark this as number one? If he hit the bridge and landed in the water, the bugger wouldn't stand a chance of being rescued. If, with a bit of luck, he had a head injury or a broken leg, he may not be found till the next day continued Maddie hopefully.

"We cannot depend on luck of any kind," stressed Ursula.

Walking on, Glenda moved away to feed a couple of horses some sugar lumps. "They are so gentle," she said.

Passing two ladies with prams. The children with them had bags of apples. The road became narrower and steeper with banking on either side blocking out the daylight. Bushes grew on each side lining the road. Tall trees grew up behind the bushes almost touching in the middle.

"Now, this looks like a good place for an unpleasant accident," said Maddie. "One would need to be very careful here," she smirked. The road now became steeper and the trees taller and thicker.

Ursula exclaimed, "Here's a lovely sharp bend. This looks like the perfect location. He could hit that tree with its roots growing out into the road. This just might be the answer. At the top of the hill is the old village. The houses are large and well back from the road. In addition, two have small copses of trees and bushes," Ursula continued. She could almost visualise it in her mind's eye.

Glenda agreed. "This is the best we can hope for."

Glenda is the best driver," Maddie surmised. "Also, she will have her taxi sign."

"We will work it all out after lunch. I'm a wee bit concerned how he is going to hit the tree if he is travelling up the way. It is a tricky one," said Ursula.

Chapter 84

All three spent as much time as possible going over that road. Ursula was a little concerned in case someone became suspicious but no one gave them a second glance.

In the flat, on Tuesday, they pooled all their information.

"It's more or less the way Glenda said. Glenda will come down the road when Maddie rings three times to say he has turned in. Maddie and I will be hard behind him. She will tailgate him while Glenda blocks him. You both flash full beam at the same time. It takes three minutes and fifty seconds from where Glenda starts to just above the big tree. It also takes four minutes and ten seconds for him to reach the tree," said Ursula.

"Maddie," said Glenda, "you will go up the hill on the wrong side of the road. That's when I close the gap. At the same time, I'll give him a quick flash of full beam." She read what she had written, checking her notebook once more.

"He will by now be going at a fair gallop," said Ursula. "Glenda, you move out to the centre of the road, giving him no time to get out of the way. So, turning the wheel at this point will take him to the tree at sixty. What do you think, ladies?"

They both just looked at her not knowing what to say.

"This is when you, Glenda, head down to the main road and the motorway. Maddie, you get up the hill as fast as you can and head home. I repeat, do not look at his car. Keep your eyes on the road." Ursula could almost see it in her mind's eye, as if she was there.

"I pray there are no other cars on that road," she said earnestly.

Maddie asked, "How will we know if it has worked?"

"Again, it's wait and see," answered Ursula. "Furthermore, I surmise we will be plagued even more with nerves this time."

"I was afraid of that, Ursula," added Maddie. "In addition, there is the timing element. We will be working to a timetable with not a lot of room for error."

"So, expect to have the jitters. We all know how edgy we were on previous nights. So brace yourselves for this one," Ursula went on.

"That's the best approach to it," agreed Glenda.

"Right then, ladies, three o'clock on Thursday. We will all meet here for the last combined assignment," finished Ursula.

Chapter 85

Three o'clock Thursday came all too soon. They had given themselves plenty of time to change, drink strong coffee and try to relax. They were as organised as it was possible to be. All three were extremely nervous. They were aware that this one was for Ursula who had been there for them throughout this whole ordeal.

"Tonight, we stay here together as we always do after a job. On Sunday we will catch up. We leave all decisions to then," Ursula told them. "We are all jittery now. Check, do we have phones all fully charged and watches at the correct time?"

"When we finish, Maddie, you go up through Dullatur and head for the motorway and home. Here."

"No bother," answered a subdued Maddie.

"You, Glenda, will go down towards the main road and again head for the motorway. Is that okay with you?" she asked.

"Yes," said a quiet Glenda.

"I repeat, do not look at his car or anything else. Do you both get that? All our nerves are bad enough," she explained. "We don't want pictures in our minds. I think we have all had enough of action replay."

They left the flat, each making for their cars. Arriving at the Coach Road, Maddie waited with Ursula at the road end while Glenda drove up the hill, at the same time putting on her dark glasses. Waiting for the four rings from Maddie, she was almost sick with fear.

Maddie saw him from quite a way off. Ringing Glenda, she sat trembling. He turned fast into the road, taking the corner so quickly he was almost on two wheels. Hell, she thought, he's in a hurry.

Quick as a flash, she was behind him, staying glued to his rear. As he neared the big tree, she spied Glenda almost in the centre of the road. She had full beam on for about thirty seconds, blocking his way. He had nowhere to move to and no time to get out of Glenda's way. She could see him twist his steering wheel in a last desperate effort to avoid the coming car. Almost at the same time, he slammed head on into the big tree. There was a very loud bang. Then silence.

Maddie and Ursula kept well in, allowing Glenda to move at lightning speed past them. Maddie and Ursula, looking straight ahead, moved quickly around him and up to the road. Heading, as instructed, for the motorway.

Oops, thought Glenda. She had a free run even as her knees were knocking her heart hammering against her ribs. Ten minutes later, she was on the motorway, taking it carefully. Only then did she realise her blouse was stuck to her back and her hands were slippery on the steering wheel.

Both Ursula and Maddie were in the flat when she arrived.

"I've never been so scared in my life as I was tonight," gasped Glenda as she fell into a seat.

"That was really hairy," said Maddie. It's not till you get back you think of all the things that could have gone wrong."

"I don't mind telling you," said Glenda, "it seemed to go that fast. All that planning and practice. Then it's over in about four minutes. Remind me, Ursula, to change the tyres on Simon's car. I put spares on in case they left traces," said Glenda.

"I can hardly remember how we managed it," said Maddie.

"Don't worry, you know you'll have flashbacks later. Some nice hot soup will help to calm you," reassured Ursula.

"Do you think we succeeded?" asked Glenda, turning to Ursula.

"No need to think of that just now," repeated Ursula.

"That was like making a movie, it didn't seem real. Everything went spot on. I can hardly believe it." Glenda babbled on. "Do you think it worked, Ursula?" she asked again.

"I don't know," Ursula replied. "No one could have survived that crash. I could hear it from where I was at the back. Eat your soup and try to settle down. Are you all right, Maddie?"

"Yes but I'm afraid to close my eyes."

"We are all as high as kites. It will be difficult to sleep tonight," she added kindly.

It was a fitful night for them all. Next morning found them all strangely quiet.

"We'll meet here Monday evening. Maybe we will be a little more composed. So, have a nice, restful weekend. Please try and relax," said Ursula as they all left.

Chapter 86

At the Monday meeting, they were all a bit more composed. Ursula made coffee and some biscuits.

"This flat has three months still paid for. So that means we have that time to clear it. "Take anything you want. Glenda, I know you would like the recliner seats for you and your mother. Has she moved in with you yet?"

"Yes," Glenda replied. "Now I have time to have time to have her wee room redecorated, she will feel much more at home. She has all her own furniture and my sisters will all muck in to help. I am really pleased. Thank you, Ursula."

"Maddie, maybe your mum may like the other recliner? You must admit they are extremely comfortable."

"Yes, she would. I'm sure she will love one. Thank you, Ursula," answered Maddie.

"All the clothes and wigs we can donate to charity shops. Some things, we will need to put on a bonfire, like gloves and scene suits. The phones we will drop in some river. All the wigs are fine. Charity shops love these for fancy dress outfits."

"We meet again in about six months for a catch up. We will see each other when we are cleaning out here. I will always be your friend and we will meet each year on our anniversary. The one for the lawyer meant so much to me, I can never forget that day in court. No one cared about Simon but we did.

"Our job here is complete. On a brighter note, these two envelopes contain what is left from our fund now that you have both acquired a taste for travel, this is a wee start up fund. Simon would have loved the whole idea. My mother left them her house in the West End. Bet she would never have believed what it was worth after over forty years.

"We have become much more than sisters or friends. Our bond is much stronger than that," she said.

"You, Ursula, have given us both justice and the semblance of a fresh start," said Maddie.

"We will both be extremely thankful to you, Ursula. We were both lost – and you found us," added Glenda.

It's over at last, thought Ursula. Thank God for that.

"By the way, ladies, I thought you might like to see today's *Herald*.

The article was brief:

Yesterday, Friday 16th October, the well-known Glasgow lawyer, Mr Campbell McIntosh, LLB, Dip LP, 42 years of age, was fatally injured in a road traffic accident while travelling home. No other vehicle was involved.

They each had their own thoughts and feelings as they read the paper in utter silence.

The End